PUFFIN BOOKS
THE NARAYANPUR INCIDENT

Shashi Deshpande was born in Dharwad, India, where she had her early education. She later moved to Bombay and Bangalore and acquired degrees in Economics and the Law, as well as a postgraduate degree in English Literature and a diploma in Journalism.

Shashi Deshpande, who has written six novels and has five short story collections to her credit, began writing children's books with her two young sons in mind, using her own childhood memories in her first book, *A Summer Adventure*. She then went on to write three more books for children, *The Narayanpur Incident* being the last.

She now lives in Bangalore with her pathologist husband.

The Narayanpur Incident

Shashi Deshpande

Illustrations by Jaideep Chakravarti

PUFFIN BOOKS

PUFFIN BOOKS
Penguin Books India (P) Ltd., 210, Chiranjiv Tower, Nehru Place,
New Delhi 110 019, India
Penguin Books Ltd., 27 Wrights Lane, London W8 5TZ, UK
Penguin Books USA Inc., 375 Hudson Street, New York, NY 10014, USA
Penguin Books Australia Ltd., Ringwood, Victoria, Australia
Penguin Books Canada Ltd., 10 Alcorn Avenue, Suite 300, Toronto,
Ontario M4V 3B2, Canada
Penguin Books (NZ) Ltd., 182-190 Wairau Road, Auckland 10, New Zealand

This book was first published by IBH Publishing Company, Bombay, in 1982.
First published by Penguin Books India (P) Ltd. 1995

Copyright © Shashi Deshpande 1995

Typeset in New Baskerville by Digital Technologies and Printing Solutions, New
Delhi

For   Ajit

Introduction

IT WAS IN 1631 that the English came to India for the purpose of trade. Then, in 1858, after the great revolt, the British Crown took over from the East India Company and India became a part of the British Empire. The British finally left India in 1947. During these ninety years, particularly the last fifty, there was a continuous struggle between Indians who wanted freedom and their British rulers. It was Mahatma Gandhi, with his strange new weapons like satyagraha, non-violence and non-cooperation, who brought the masses of India into the freedom struggle. But the British refused to yield. Even when the Second World War broke out and Britain had to fight desperately for her own survival, she did not change her attitude towards India. India's patience was also wearing thin. It was then, on 8 August 1942 in Bombay, that the AICC session passed the famous 'Quit India' resolution. 'Quit India and give us our freedom,' India was calling.

The Government's reply to this was to arrest all the leaders in the early hours of 9 August 1942 and take them away secretly to different jails. When the news spread, the people were furious. With no leaders to guide them or to tell them what to do, the people rose in protest on their own. Some took the Gandhian way of protesting—organising hartals and meetings, and courting arrest. Others were more violent. Government property, like railway stations and post offices, were attacked and burnt. On its part, the government hit back ruthlessly, with arrests, flogging, and firing on unarmed crowds.

Shashi Deshpande

This then was the 1942 Quit India Movement which forms the background to this story. Only forty years separate us from this movement. Nevertheless, for some reason, it seems to belong to quite another age. So much so that when I spoke to my young sons about my plan to write a book based on this movement and narrated some of the incidents that inspired me, they were incredulous. 'You must be exaggerating,' they said. 'Heroism! Bravery! In our country!'

I am sure there are many youngsters like them who believe that heroism has no place in our lives any more. We feel that we have to go far back in time to find heroes and heroines. And yet, the fact is that in 1942 hundreds and thousands of ordinary people threw themselves into the struggle, courageously facing all the terrible consequences. This is what makes the 1942 Movement unique—the courage and sacrifices of so many ordinary people.

Let me assure you that most of the incidents you will read of in this book did, in fact, happen. And while Narayanpur, as also Mohan, Babu, Manju, Vasant, Shanti and all the others are entirely my own creations, the incident with which this book ends did take place in a small village. What started as a children's game ended in tragedy and the whole village had to pay for it. Bhima too, is not real, but there were many like him who paid with their lives for the country's freedom. To all these brave people who took part in this last battle for freedom, I dedicate this book.

Finally, I would like to thank my parents for making available to me all the material on the movement which they had with them, and my husband for so patiently going through all the Kannada documents with me.

Bangalore, 1981   *Shashi Deshpande*

I

SOMETHING WAS UP, there was no doubt about it at all.
First, there had been all those visitors with whom Appa had
been talking for nearly two hours. Amma had waited ages
for Appa to come and join them for dinner. Finally she had
said, 'Manju, Babu, come and have your dinner.'

'And Appa?'

'Oh, he'll have his later.'

But Amma's mind was far away, Babu noticed, for the
dal had no salt in it, and Manju's roti had been burnt.

'Amma, look!' Manju had pointed accusingly at her roti.

'Oh, what a pity!' Amma had said coolly, as if it didn't
really matter.

And now, as Babu lay in bed trying to get to sleep, he
could still hear the voices going on and on. Mohan's bed
was empty—he was with the others. Lucky Mohan, to be part
of everything that was going on. Five years more before
Babu could be as old as Mohan was now. How immensely
long five years seemed! Anyway, thank goodness Manju
was two years younger than him. Terrible to be the
youngest.

He had just dropped off when the scraping of a chair
woke him up.

'Mohan?' he mumbled, opening his eyes with difficulty.

'Hello? Still awake? What's the matter?'

'Mohan, what's happening?'

'What do you mean?'

'All those people, and all that talk . . . . Is something
happening?'

'You know, Babu,' Mohan's voice was suddenly muffled

and his head disappeared as he pulled his shirt over his head, 'I think,' his head reappeared, 'Amma can throw away all the knives in this house.'

'Knives?'

Babu, fully awake now, was bewildered. What had knives to do with anything? 'But why?'

'Because your nose seems to be sharper than any knife. Don't go poking it into matters that have nothing to do with you.'

'Yah! Joke! Anyway, a sharp nose is better than a squashed one,' Babu retorted.

'Mmmmm,' Mohan tapped his own nose thoughtfully, then asked with a grin, 'you mean like mine? Don't be cheeky, fellow, or else you won't get my bike.'

'Who wants your bike?'

'You! That's who!'

Babu wriggled in his bed and said, changing the subject, 'Oh, come on, Mohan, be a sport and tell me what's going on.'

'It's the AICC session in Bombay today. Don't you know we're all waiting for news of what's being decided there?'

'Oh, that!'

It sounded too dull and tame a thing to get excited about; but then, their family was like that. Appa, Amma and Mohan were all so involved with the Congress, Gandhiji and Swaraj and all such things that an AICC session was bound to excite them.

'Is that all?' he asked with a yawn and snuggled back under his blanket. The steady drip of the rain was soothing. 'Why make such a fuss about that?'

But Mohan, settling himself with squeaks and creaks in his own bed, ignored Babu's question. 'I hope we get some news tomorrow morning,' he mumbled before drawing his blanket over his head.

News came very early, much earlier than they had expected. Even before the milkmen began their morning rounds, there was a loud banging on the front door.

Babu opened his eyes, coming out of a chaotic dream, not sure whether he was still dreaming or awake. He heard the sound of the front door being opened, then a confused jumble of voices. Properly awake now, he ran out into the small hall where Mohan, Appa and Appa's friend—the editor of the local newspaper—were laughing and talking about something.

'What is it, Appa? What's happened?' Babu asked the question three times before Mohan turned round and gave him a hard slap on the back.

'Oh there you are, Babu. Have you heard? Are you ready?'

'For what?' Babu asked, adding almost immediately, 'Yes, I'm ready.'

'To do or die?'

Babu's mouth fell open. He stared at Mohan in astonishment. What did it mean? Was Mohan making fun of him? Would no one explain, he thought indignantly. Appa's friend—they called him Dinkar-kaka—was drinking the water Amma had just got for him.

Appa, noticing Babu's face, gave him one of his quick, rare smiles and said, 'Dinkar has been telling us about the AICC resolution in Bombay yesterday. They've passed a resolution asking the British to quit India.' Appa's eyes had that faraway look and now it was as if he had forgotten he was talking to Babu. 'Quit India,' he said softly, as if tasting the words.

'And so, Appa?' Babu demanded.

'And so . . . ' Appa came back from wherever he'd gone, 'we're going to have a mass civil disobedience movement. You know what that means.'

'Fighting the British,' Babu said promptly. 'But no guns.'

'There you are,' Appa said, as if immensely satisfied with Babu's reply. 'He's put it in a nutshell.'

'He isn't your son for nothing,' Amma said, taking the empty glass from Dinkar-kaka.

'But why did Mohan ask me to get ready to do or die?'

'Do or die,' Mohan repeated. The words seemed to please him as much as Babu's reply had pleased Appa. 'That's what the Mahatma has asked us to do.'

'Listen.' Dinkar-kaka pulled out a piece of paper from a bulky file he was carrying. 'I'll read it out to you—I've got the very words. This is what Gandhiji said: "Here is a mantra . . . a short one I give you. We shall do or die. We shall either free India or die in the attempt. We shall not live to see the perpetration of slavery."'

Dinkar-kaka's voice was choked as he came to the end. Amma standing at the door, the glass still in her hand, wiped her eyes with the end of her sari. Appa looked solemn. 'Hurrah! Out with the British. Indians never, never, never shall be slaves,' Mohan sang in a funny tune as if it were an English song. Appa, Amma and Dinkar-kaka laughed at him, but Babu, as excited as Mohan now, jumped up and down, shouting, 'Never, never, never. Oh, Mohan, are we really going to do it?'

'Yes, young fellow.'

'I'm joining this time.'

'You will,' Mohan rumpled his hair. 'No more timid little gestures this time—picketing, hartals, satyagraha and going to jail tamely. We're going all out this time.'

'Now, Mohan,' Appa began sternly, wiping his glasses.

'You don't seem to realize, Appa, that force is the only thing the British will understand and respect . . . . '

'Now, listen . . . ' Appa looked worried and Amma looked anxiously from him to Mohan. Another argument! Babu, who was only fourteen—thirteen really, fourteen in seven more months—wondered how Mohan, even though he was eighteen, could argue so much with Appa. Babu went back into his room as the arguments began, but it was just impossible to go back to sleep as Amma suggested he do.

Fight against the British—it sounded splendid. But how

was one to do it? Specially when one wasn't supposed to use guns or any weapons at all? Appa said that Gandhiji's way was the right way. Satyagraha and hartals were infinitely better than guns and battles, he insisted. 'We're bound to win in the end, and it's a better way of winning.'

But, Babu thought wistfully, a bit of a real fight would be fun. And this time it would be a real fight. If it was, and he was allowed to take part . . . .

Suddenly he remembered Manju. She was still sleeping and knew nothing of what had happened. He ought to wake her up and tell her about it. He would also tell her that Mohan had promised him he could take part in it this time.

'And me?' she would be sure to ask jealously.

'Oh, what can you do?' he would say casually. 'You're only a girl.'

He also knew what Manju's reply to that would be. 'So what?'

Manju was sleeping, all curled up as usual, hugging her pillow tightly. Babu shook her roughly: 'Manju, hey Manju.'

After a dozen shakes, she mumbled sleepily, her eyes tightly closed, 'Oh, go away, I'll get up in a minute.'

'Get up, Manju, such exciting news.'

'Mmmph,' she mumbled, and turning over, went right back to sleep.

Babu came back to his own bed. As he lay there, wonderful pictures danced in front of his eyes. He, Babu, defying a whole battalion of soldiers all by himself. And from that he slowly drifted into a dream in which Appa was saying, 'Now, boys, the square root of . . . .'

When Amma woke him up, Manju was already awake. She rushed to him asking him, 'Babu, have you heard the news?'

'Hours ago,' Babu said contemptuously, rolling up his mattress. 'I was awake half the night and heard it long before you did.'

'Half the night? Don't exaggerate.'

'Ask Amma if you don't believe me. Well, not half the night . . . '

'Children, don't waste time. Babu, do you know what the time is? You'll be late if you don't hurry.'

Babu, after one look at the time, danced around in a frenzy trying to get ready. Appa had left earlier. He taught in Babu's school, and that wasn't such a good thing as far as Babu was concerned. The smallest lapse on Babu's part—like not doing his homework or being late for school—and the masters pounced on him, as if to say: 'Just because you're a master's son, don't imagine you can escape!' And at home Appa would be waiting with reproachful eyes.

By the time Babu and Manju set off for school, they had forgotten all about the early morning excitement and were thinking of other things. Manju was worried about her music class that day. Manju hated singing and the music teacher was an irritable woman who, for some reason, seemed to dislike Manju specially. Music classes were a real misery for her.

Babu was thinking of the forthcoming football match against the government school. He wasn't in the team, but hoped to be in it some time. Last year the government school had defeated them. This year they hoped to have their revenge.

In school, however, the excitement began all over again. Babu had just written the date neatly in the margin— 9-8-1942—for the first period, when there was an interruption. Their master—it was a History period—was taking attendance when another master rushed in and started whispering excitedly. The boys watched curiously.

Murali, sitting next to Babu, jabbed him in the side with his sharp elbow and said, 'We're going to have a holiday.'

'What for?'

'Perhaps Ranganath Sir is dead,' Murali grinned.

Ranganath Sir taught them Sanskrit and had a sarcastic tongue which he used freely on the irresponsible Murali.

'Or perhaps the war is over,' another boy said, at which Shridhar, who was crazy about joining the Army and taking part in the war, retorted, 'Impossible! They're going to wait for me. They've promised me.'

'Then,' Murali's grin became even wider, 'Churchill must be dead.'

Babu, who knew that their school—a private school and not a government one—would not give a holiday for any such reason, wondered as he saw the serious faces of the two masters.

As the boys' whispers became louder, with Murali's voice clearly saying, 'It's a holiday, I bet it's a holiday', the other master went out and their master said loudly, rapping the table with the back of the duster, 'Silence, boys. We're not having classes today. You can go home.'

The sheer unexpectedness of it kept the boys silent for a minute. Then Murali came out of it exclaiming, 'I knew it. I told you so. Who's dead, sir? Is it Churchill? Or Stalin?'

'Sssh, quiet, boy. Don't let your tongue run away with you. Just go home quietly, all of you.'

Calmly he began gathering his books as if that was it! But the boys wouldn't let him off so easily. They rushed to him, clamouring for more information.

'Sir, what is it? What's happened? Why are we having a holiday?'

'The war is over, the war is over, Hitler has surrendered,' someone said loudly.

'Sssh, less noise, boys. This has nothing to do with the war. It's not even our war, by the way. I hope you boys remember that. We were not asked, were we, whether we wanted to be part of it? We were just dragged into it.'

This was what Appa said as well. In fact, all the masters in this school were nationalists, patriots and followers of Gandhi.

'Now, just disperse quietly. No noise, remember.'

The master's voice was hushed, not as forceful as usual, and Babu could sense that he was upset. Something had happened.

'Please, sir,' he pleaded, 'what has happened?'

The master, ready to leave, his books tucked under his arm, stopped at the door, looked at Babu and the other boys, and then said, 'Yes, I think you should know. The Mahatma has been arrested.'

The voices stopped suddenly as if someone had cut into them with a knife.

'Not just him. Many others have been arrested too. Nehru, Kripalani, Azad, Patel, Rajendra Prasad and God knows how many others. We don't have all the news yet. There's going to be a hartal today to protest against these arrests. That's why the Headmaster has decided to close the school today. Just go home quietly now and don't get involved in any trouble.'

Something happened to Babu then. As if someone had set off an alarm within him, telling him that it had begun. It was a strange feeling he could never describe to others. He didn't really understand it himself, but it made him feel very solemn. He walked out of school very subdued. As a matter of fact, all the boys were quiet. There was no pushing, no shoving, no loud cries of joy in spite of the unexpected holiday.

Babu and his special friend, Gopya, were out of the school compound when Babu suddenly remembered Manju. She would be having a holiday too. Better to take her along with him if there was going to be any trouble. The first thing Amma would ask him when he reached home would be, 'Where's Manju?'

'You go ahead, Gopya,' he said. 'I'll be with you in a minute.'

Manju's school was really part of theirs, but housed in a separate and smaller building, just across the road. Of course, Babu wouldn't go inside the girls' school, no, not even if anyone gave him a thousand rupees. Once he had been forced to go there when Manju had suddenly fallen ill and he had to take her home. He could still remember how terrible it had felt to be in the midst of so many girls, all of whom looked, from the way they giggled, as if they found him extremely funny.

As he loitered uncomfortably outside the gate, he saw Manju running out, her satchel swinging wildly, her pigtail flying behind her, her long skirts rustling. 'Babu, we have a holiday, we have a holiday.'

'I know that.' He hurried her away. He could see the girls pouring out. 'Let's get home fast. Our master said there may be trouble.'

'Trouble? What trouble?'

'There is a hartal today.'

'Oh! And will it make the British let Gandhiji and the others out of jail?' she asked seriously.

'Will what make whom do what?' Gopya, with whom they had just caught up, asked confusingly. But Babu knew what he meant.

'She wants to know if the hartal will make the British release Gandhi. As if it will! We've got to fight the British properly this time. Mohan says so.'

'Let's join in, Babu,' Gopya said enthusiastically.

'We will. Mohan promised me we can this time.'

Yes, it was all coming back now, all the things that had not been only a dream, after all.

'Mohan says it's going to be a real struggle this time, not just hartals, satyagrahas and all that. The Mahatma himself told us to do or die. Mohan told me that.'

Gopya's eyes lit up. 'Come on, Babu, let's join the struggle. I'm tired of school and studies. And the masters scolding me in school and my father scolding me at home. I'm sick of it all. Let's get out before the exams,' he added with a grin.

'Me too,' Manju said. 'I'm joining also.'

'You!' Gopya hooted with laughter. 'As if girls can fight. They cry for the smallest things.'

'Huh!' Manju said angrily. 'Girls can do anything, Amma says. Look at Sarojini Naidu. Look at Kamala Nehru. And . . . '

'The Rani of Jhansi,' Babu completed the sentence for her. 'Okay, Manju, you too.'

'I say, look at that!' Gopya suddenly exclaimed, pointing a finger.

They were just outside the police station now and there were more police there than they had ever seen before. Officers too, trim and armed with short lathis, revolvers at their waists. Appa called the police 'traitors', and so, for Babu and Manju too they were the enemy. The three children stood there on the dusty road and stared at the policemen. Getting ready, obviously. But for what? An officer passing them said, not unkindly, 'Now, children, don't loiter on the roads. Go home.'

Suddenly Manju screamed: 'Mohan, Mohananna.'

Yes, there he was with a friend, both of them on bikes.

'Mohan take me with you, let me come with you,' Manju pleaded.

Mohan would never have refused either Babu or Manju a ride on the bike with him. Today, to their surprise, he was curt. 'No, not now, Manju. Babu, go home fast. Amma will be worried about the two of you. Gopya, you must get home quickly too.'

As he rode away, he called back over his shoulder, 'Tell Amma not to worry about me.'

And off he went, head bent low, crouched over the handlebar, pedalling hard until he caught up with his friend. The two of them turned off into a lane and were lost to sight.

II

'THANK GOD, YOU'RE home,' Amma said.

'Amma do you know what's happened?'

'I heard the news soon after you left for school. It's a terrible thing. I never thought they'd be such utter fools.'

'Who, Amma?' Manju asked curiously.

'The British. Imagine arresting the one man who could have controlled the people!' Her eyebrows were knit in a frown, her eyes were worried. 'Have you seen Mohan?' she asked abruptly, changing the subject.

'Yes, he went with a friend into the lane where the basket-makers live.'

'Oh!' She bit her lip. 'And Appa?'

'I don't know. I never saw him.'

Appa taught only the two senior classes and Babu rarely met him in school.

'There's nothing we can do but wait for them, then.'

'Amma, I'm hungry,' Babu protested.

'He's always hungry,' Manju said scornfully.

'Why not? I'm a growing boy,' Babu retorted.

'I didn't mean wait for lunch,' Amma said with a smile. 'I meant we have to wait to know what's happening. Come on, wash up and have your lunch.'

After lunch Babu wanted to rush out and see what was going on, but Amma wouldn't allow him to. So the three of them stayed at home, waiting for something, anything. At one time they thought they heard faint shouts, but these soon faded away. Later, it was so hushed and silent that it could have been the dead of night. It was eerie. Once a neighbour came and spoke to Amma in whispers.

'What is it?' Babu asked impatiently.

'There's a hartal,' Amma told them, her face sober. 'All the shops are closed, all schools and colleges too. Everything, except the government offices.'

'Oh, how I wish Appa would come home soon.'

But it was Mohan who came home first. He fell off his bike, looking tense and excited. 'Appa? he asked panting.

'He hasn't come as yet.'

'Thank goodness. Do you know where he is?'

'No. Why, what's the matter?'

'He's going to be arrested.'

Babu and Manju stared at Mohan in horror.

'There have been plenty of arrests already.'

'Who?'

Mohan told Amma some of the names which included Dinkar-kaka. 'And his press has been closed down,' Mohan went on. 'It's too bad. He was going to publish the Mahatma's speech. They're arresting the leaders everywhere. Appa mustn't let them find him. I've got to warn him. Where do you think he'll be?'

'I really don't know, Mohan.' Amma seemed calm and unmoved, but Manju noticed that her fingers, which went up to smooth her hair, were trembling slightly. 'You can try that place—you know the one above the bookshop? They meet there sometimes.'

'Okay.' And Mohan clambered on to his bike at once.

'And come back soon.'

Mohan just had time for a backward wave of his hand.

'Will they really arrest Appa?' Manju asked, rather shakily. You heard about other people being arrested, but when it was your own father—and a father so gentle that he rarely raised his voice . . . .

'If they're arresting all the leaders, I suppose they'll take him as well. There is nothing we can do about it.'

'But Amma,' Babu said impatiently, 'you heard what Mohan said. Surely he can escape?'

'Where to?' Amma asked simply, and Babu and Manju had no answer to that.

Mohan returned in a short while. 'Well?' Amma asked.

Mohan shook his head dumbly. He took off his slippers and came in. 'I couldn't meet him, but I sent him a message asking him to keep away.'

'What for, Mohan? How long can he keep away?'

'I don't know, but he mustn't let himself get arrested.' Mohan clenched his jaw. 'They want us to be left without leaders, they want us to get confused. And we shouldn't let them do that.'

As he ate his food, Mohan told them about the hartal. 'It was grand,' he said, his face lighting up. 'Wonderful! If only we could always be like this. We didn't even have to go round asking the shopkeepers to close their shops. Most of them did it on their own the minute they heard of the Mahatma's arrest. The police were hoping for some trouble, for a chance to beat up people, to harass them. But did they get it?' Mohan grinned. 'No, they didn't. It was a total, peaceful hartal. I've never seen the market like that. It was fantastic—even the tongawalas and the coolies joined in. That's the way to show the British we're all in it and we mean business.'

The long hand of the grandfather clock seemed to move like a snail as they waited for Appa and afternoon passed into evening. Dinner time, bedtime—and still no Appa. Finally they had their dinner and tried to settle down in their beds.

'Mohan, do you think Appa has escaped?' Babu asked.

'Don't know, Babu. Let's wait and see. I have a feeling he'll come home some time.'

He did come that night. Babu came out of his sleep some time during the night. Something had disturbed him, some sound. What was it? There it was again. A soft tap at the window. Babu's throat went tight with fear. Then, as the tap was repeated, he sprang up and asked, 'What? Who's there?'

'Babu, it's me. Appa. Go quietly and open the back door. Don't switch on any light. Wake Amma up, quietly, mind.'

As Babu moved into the central room, Amma called out, 'What is it? Babu? Mohan?'

'Amma, Appa is here. He says to open the back door and not to switch on any lights.'

Babu softly unbolted the back door and Appa came in. Three or four men followed him in and the last man softly bolted the door again. Mohan and Amma were there too, and the small back passage, with its musty smell of drying clothes and leftover food, seemed crowded with people and the sounds of breathing.

'Let's go in,' Appa said softly. 'Careful,' he warned, 'there are vessels in that corner.'

They all went into Babu's and Mohan's room. 'Babu,' Appa said, 'you go in with Amma and Manju.'

But Babu pretended he hadn't heard Appa—he wasn't going to be left out. Quietly he sneaked in. Mohan had rolled up Babu's mattress and the men settled down on the ground. Babu was edging towards Mohan's bed when Appa said, 'All right, Babu, you can sleep on Mohan's bed. But don't listen. Just go to sleep.'

'All right,' Babu said thankfully, diving under Mohan's blanket. He dutifully closed his eyes—well, he was trying to go to sleep, but it wasn't his fault that sleep wouldn't come. And how could he help listening unless he put his fingers in his ears? He tried putting his fingers in his ears and taking them out again, so that the low sounds came and went in waves. It was like going into a tunnel and coming out again. But it was too uncomfortable to keep up for long. Finally, he just lay quietly, letting his ears pick up whatever they could.

Which was not much, really, for the men sat in a huddle and spoke in soft voices. Occasionally, if one of them forgot to speak softly, the others immediately hushed him. But Babu's sharp ears could make out that there was some sort of an argument going on about what to do next. There seemed to be a difference of opinion and some confusion. One of the men—he seemed fairly young from his voice—said there was no point at all in everyone getting arrested and going to jail. The point was to stay out, be active and trouble the government as much as they could. Never mind how they did this, they just had to go all out now.

'Hear, hear,' Mohan said softly.

'Mohan,' Appa said in exasperation, 'you shouldn't be here at all.'

And Mohan replied, almost rudely, 'Well, if the lot of you go and settle down tamely in jail, like circus tigers ...'

Babu suddenly laughed out loud at the idea of Appa being a circus tiger, but luckily no one heard him.

'... it's we who'll have to do something, so how can you keep me out anyway?'

Appa and the others—one of them, Babu realized with a shock, was their Headmaster—said they had to follow what Gandhiji had taught them. Which meant peaceful demonstrations, hartals, satyagrahas, processions, etc. Certainly no violence. Going quietly to jail if arrested.

'Tchah!' the young voice said disgustedly.

'Now, Sadanand,' Appa patiently began.

The arguments went on and on. Babu dozed off at some time. Once he opened his eyes and saw that the moonlight was now streaming in through the window, neatly dissected by the window bars.

And then Babu really slept. He woke up to find Mohan sleeping peacefully on a mattress on the floor. There was no one else in the room. Appa? The others? 'Mohan,' he called out loudly.

It was Amma who came in, saying, 'Babu, are you awake?'

Babu looked round once again before asking, 'Appa?'

'Sssh, they've gone.'

'Where, Amma?'

'I don't know.'

Mohan now woke up abruptly, pushed his two hands through his hair, and said irritably, 'Good God! What's going on, Amma? Why are you jabbering away, Babu? You woke me up.' Then he gave an enormous yawn and said, 'I've hardly slept.'

'Look, Babu,' Amma came and sat on the bed, looking at him with a serious face, 'you're not to tell anyone that Appa was here. Or the others, either. Nobody came here and you know nothing. Okay?'

'Why?' Babu sat up straight and stared at Amma. 'Are they going to arrest Appa?'

'Of course.' Mohan made a face. 'And Appa's going to let himself be arrested.' He saw Amma's face and said impatiently, 'It's all right, Amma. Let him know about it. After all, he's thirteen.'

'Fourteen,' Babu corrected him.

'Okay, fourteen. But even if you're fourteen, I can still smack you if you blab a word of this to anyone.'

Babu was furious. 'Blab? Me? What do you think I am? A silly kid?'

Babu could feel his ears getting hot, as they always did when he was angry. His voice turned squeaky—a nasty habit, recently acquired—and Mohan couldn't help grinning.

'Okay, okay. Now listen . . . oh, let me tell him, Amma; Babu's a sensible chap. Appa is going to get himself arrested today.'

'Where? When?'

'There's going to be a public meeting to protest against the arrests. Appa is going to speak. They'll be sure to arrest him as soon as they see him. In the meantime he's going to stay hidden.'

'And the others?'

'What others?' Mohan asked blankly and Babu, after a moment's surprise, understood. 'That's right,' he said with a grin. 'There were no others.'

'If only,' Mohan said, frowning moodily, giving the rolled-up mattress a little kick, 'if only Appa would have agreed to go underground, he'd have been of much more use to the movement.'

Going underground—this was a phrase Babu and Manju were to hear again and again after that day. Now it meant nothing to Babu, though later he realized its true meaning. It meant going into hiding to escape arrest. So many men and women did it—hiding in old temples, in other people's homes, in jungles, moving from place to place to evade the police—all this so that they could carry on the fight. But Appa would not be one of them.

'Anyway,' Amma said, 'school for you, boy.'

'School?' Babu was shocked.

'Yes, that's your job. Yours and Manju's. And Mohan has to go to college.'

'All right, Amma, I'm going. I'm going.'

Something in Mohan's face and eyes told Babu that he was planning something; yes, he had something up his sleeve. But he would never tell what it was. Babu would have to wait to know about it.

'What about Manju, Amma?' Babu suddenly remembered. 'Can we tell her Appa was here last night?'

'She knows about it. Appa woke her up before leaving.'

Babu felt a bit jealous. Appa hadn't woken him up.

'You'd just fallen asleep,' Amma said quickly, as if she had guessed Babu's thoughts. 'He didn't want to disturb you all over again.'

'School,' Babu grumbled as Manju and he walked to school. 'Is there nothing else for us?'

Manju stopped and stared at Babu. He wasn't normally a grumbler. 'What do you want to do?'

'Something. Anything. Take part in the movement. Fight the British.'

'How? With your catapult? Ha! ha!'

Babu scowled at her. 'Stop braying like an ass. And just

you wait and see. Gopya,' he yelled. They were now outside Gopya's house. 'Hey, Gopya.'

Gopya ran out, followed by his mother's cry, 'Gopya, take your bag. Are you going to school without your books?'

Gopya made a face, ran in and ran out in a flash, with his bag this time. 'I say, Babu,' he began in a rush before Babu or Manju could say a word. 'You know what happened yesterday?' His eyes were glittering with excitement. 'They're arresting people left and right. They arrested my mother's uncle yesterday. They took him to jail,' Gopya boasted. 'I saw them—the police. They came to our house searching for him. They found him later. My mother cried a lot.'

Babu found it hard to listen to Gopya's bragging when he knew so much more himself. Far more exciting things. But no, he couldn't reveal them. Manju listened in silence too, her eyes sharing their secret with Babu. Oh, it was hard to keep silent. Gopya found Babu's silence strange too—when he noticed it, that is. 'What's wrong with you?' he asked.

'With me?'

'Are you sick or something?'

'No,' Babu replied curtly.

'He doesn't want to go to school,' Manju burst out. 'He wants to go and fight the British.'

'I wish I could do that myself,' Gopya sighed heavily and kicked a stone hard, looking both fierce and wistful at the same time.

'But Appa said we've got to go to school, do our work, study hard and be prepared . . . .'

'When did Appa say that?' Babu asked Manju suspiciously.

'Why, last . . . I mean, last month,' Manju corrected herself, hoping Gopya hadn't noticed.

'Well, it's easy for Appa to say these things. He's a teacher, isn't he? He's got to say such things. But I hate the idea of just going to school,' Babu said moodily.

When they reached school they found an unusual commotion instead of the usual crowd of school-going children. There seemed to be many older boys there today, who looked like college students.

'What's happened? What's the matter?' Gopya asked, his voice shrill and excited.

'They've arrested our Headmaster,' someone shouted over the din.

The three of them rushed to get closer, Manju too, for the girls were here as well. Babu, trying to wriggle into the crowd, saw some boys dragging out a scarred bench. A young master from Babu's school suddenly jumped on to it, even before the boys had put it down, so that he had to leap about for a moment, trying to balance himself.

'Mahatma Gandhi ki jai,' he called out.

'Mahatma Gandhi ki jai,' the children called back.

Now there was even more confusion, more jostling and pushing. Police appeared out of nowhere, and all at once there was a police officer standing on the bench instead of the master. He held something in one hand which was raised above his head. Crack, crack, the sounds rang through the air, sharp and loud. And in the silence that followed, the officer's voice was clearly heard. 'Go home, all of you. We don't want any trouble. Disperse immediately.' And then he disappeared as he stepped off the bench.

'What do we do now?' Gopya asked Babu.

'I don't know.'

'Mahatma Gandhi ki jai,' the cry came again, defiantly, from a group of older boys. There was a scuffle. A thick haze of dust rose from the ground, churned up by the many feet. It got into their noses and their eyes. Babu sneezed repeatedly and rubbed his eyes furiously. When he opened them he saw objects rising and falling in the air. Once more there was a series of sharp sounds. Lathis! Babu saw two or three boys fall to the ground.

The police were everywhere. There was a rush for the school building. A group of girls were running the other way, towards their own school. Babu noticed the Art Master running behind them, one hand holding up his dhoti, the other holding his cap, his coat flapping about him. He looked ridiculous, but Babu had only a moment to think of this for he was caught in the crowd moving into their own school building. He didn't want to go in, but there was nothing he could do about it. He was jammed between the boys and willy-nilly found himself inside. Some boys were fleeing down the corridors, but Babu wanted to get out and see what was happening. One of the masters had stationed himself at the end of the corridor to prevent the boys from going out. He saw Babu trying to go back and said, 'No, you can't. Go to your classroom and stay there.'

Babu quietly went to the side of the building and climbed out of a small window which led outside. He jumped down and found himself in a small, dark recess between the walls of two classrooms. He heard the sound of running footsteps. Two—no, there were three—boys ran past, closely pursued by a police officer, his face ugly in anger. Even as Babu watched, the police officer caught up with them. Crack, crack, the lathi came down on a boy's shoulder. He fell. The other two leaped over the low wall of the cycle shed and disappeared. The police officer, instead of chasing them, continued to rain blows on the boy lying on the ground. The boy screamed in pain. As if satisfied, the officer was about to move away when something hit him from behind.

It was Babu. He had watched in unbelieving horror when the man had hit the boy. His horror had changed into fury when he saw the man continue to hit the boy who lay screaming on the ground. To hit a boy who was already hurt! Babu saw red. He charged forward, his anger driving him blindly on. He hit the officer with the only weapon he had—his satchel, which contained all his books. But he put all his strength into the blow. Even that would scarcely have hurt the man if he hadn't been taken utterly by surprise and lost his balance. He fell over the injured boy, hit his head with a loud sound against the low wall of the cycle shed and lay still, his body lying over and across the boy's.

Babu stood transfixed in horror. What had he done? Had he killed the man? His mouth went dry, he felt there was something choking him. There were footsteps behind him. Babu turned round, scared, and then relief lit up his face.

'Mohan! Thank God, it's you!'

'Babu, what are you doing here? What's happened? What on earth . . . ?' Mohan stared in bewilderment at the two figures lying on the ground. The officer lay silent, but the boy had begun groaning.

'I hit him—the policeman,' Babu explained, stammering in his excitement. 'And he fell down. And Mohan, that poor chap is hurt—the police fellow hit him—and so I hit the man—and oh, Mohan, do you think he's dead?'

Mohan, listening in amazement, burst into laughter now. 'Dead? Not he! They've got thick skulls, these chaps. He must only be stunned. He'll come out of it soon enough. Here, help me to get him off this poor fellow. And then, you get away from here. Scoot—as fast as you can.'

The policeman felt like a rock, heavy and inert. Thank God, he was still unconscious. They slid him off the injured boy and Mohan, kneeling down, asked, 'Did he see you?'

'Who? The policeman? No, he didn't. I was behind him.'

'Good. Get out now. Fast. Go straight home.'

'And you? And this chap?'

'I'll deal with all that. You get away first.'

Mohan was still bending over the boy when Babu, who had turned away, heard him call out urgently, 'Babu!' Mohan held Babu's school bag in his hand. 'Here, you forgot this. Straight home, understand!' There was excitement in Mohan's face and voice. 'Home as fast as you

Shashi Deshpande

can,' he said emphatically, looking Babu straight in the face.
Babu nodded and took his bag from Mohan. 'Go on then.
Run.'

Babu, his bag slung over his shoulder, his feet kicking
up the dust as he ran, headed straight home as Mohan had
ordered.

III

HOME AT LAST! Babu flung himself in, startling Amma who was in the hall. He wiped his face with his sleeve and threw his bag away. It fell in the corner with a clatter.

'Babu, what's the matter? And don't treat your bag that way!'

'Amma, they've arrested our Headmaster.'

Amma, who had been about to pick up Babu's bag, straightened up without it and said, 'What!'

'Yes, and the boys were all out on the ground shouting "Mahatma Gandhi ki jai" and the police came . . . .' And so it all poured out, ending up with the policeman's fall and Mohan's timely intervention.

When he finished, Amma, who had an amused look in her eyes, though she kept her face grave, clicked her tongue and said, 'Hotheads, all of you! And where's Manju? Fighting some policeman too, I suppose!'

'I don't know, Amma. She'll turn up, don't worry,' he reassured Amma breezily.

'I'm not worried about her. I'm worried about the police and the British government.' And only then did the gravity of her face give way to laughter.

Manju turned up in a short while with some exciting news of her own. 'Amma, no school for us. The police have locked it up,' she said, putting her bag neatly away.

'What do you mean?'

'The police have locked up both the schools, Babu's and ours. And we can't go to school ever any more.'

Babu stared at her in astonishment. 'What rot!' he said at last. 'As if they could do that!'

'It isn't rot. I'm telling you they have. Our Sumitra-bai was telling us . . . '

'Fat lot your Sumitra-bai knows!'

'She knows more than you do anyway.'

'Children! Children!'

However, when Mohan returned, Babu found that what Manju had told them was true.

'They've arrested the Headmaster,' Mohan told Amma. 'And one or two other masters as well. They've taken away papers and files from both the schools and closed them down. They say the schools have been carrying on subversive activities.'

'And what does "subversive" mean, Mohan?' Manju asked.

'It means the schools have been trying to throw out the British. And why shouldn't we? When they do it in Europe against the Germans, it's wonderful. When we do it, it's treason.' Mohan was getting excited again.

'Anyway,' Babu sighed in satisfaction, 'no more school.'

'Lucky kids,' Mohan grinned, forgetting his anger for a moment.

'Isn't it wonderful?' Babu asked with a broad smile.

But later, he wondered whether he liked the idea of school being closed down just because the police said so. No, it didn't feel very nice. As for Manju, who enjoyed her studies, she felt a little sorry at the idea of not going to school. And there were all her friends—she would miss them.

'Babu,' Mohan now said abruptly, dropping his jocular tone, 'where's your bag?'

'My bag?' Babu said, looking around vaguely. 'Why, there it is.' It still lay forlornly in the corner where he had thrown it.

'Oh good!' And Mohan pounced on it.

'Why do you want my bag, Mohan? Oooh!' Babu took in a deep breath when he saw what Mohan had taken out of the bag.

Amma and Manju stared in silent bewilderment. It was Babu who found his voice first. 'Mohan, where did you get *that*!'

Mohan looked up for the first time from what he held in his hand.

'Mohan!' Amma's voice was sharp and cutting. 'How did that come here?'

'It was in Babu's bag,' Manju said.

It was a revolver—a heavy, large one.

'Babu knocked a policeman down,' Mohan said softly, his eyes watching Amma anxiously.

'Oh!' Manju said, quickly understanding. 'And this is his.'

'You picked it up and put it in my bag,' Babu went on, as if completing a song.

'Yes, that's right. It was too good a chance to miss.'

Amma looked upset and angry. 'But why, Mohan? Why do you need these things? These are not the weapons we're going to use. Or, are you?' she asked suspiciously.

'But Amma, we've got to defend ourselves. We're not going to let them beat us, knock us about, push us around, make us crawl in our own country! Look what they did today!'

'Yes, Amma, it was horrible.' Manju's face was angry. 'A girl from our school got badly hurt. She wasn't doing anything. She was just scared and trying to run away. A policeman hit her so hard, her arm is broken.'

'And Amma, you should have seen the policeman I knocked down, the way he was hitting the poor boy . . .'

'Good Heavens!' Amma put her hands to her ears. 'All in it together, I see. I told you, Babu, didn't I, that the days of the British in this country are numbered?' Then suddenly she became serious again. 'Mohan, promise me you won't use it.'

Mohan's face fell. 'What's the use of it then?' he asked reasonably. 'Only in defence, Amma, only in defence,' he

26

wheedled. 'And I'm not going to keep it with me anyway. I'm going to pass it on.'

'Sadanand, I suppose.' Amma's voice was disapproving. 'You'll be giving it to him, won't you?'

'Amma, forget it,' Mohan said irritably.

'Who's Sadanand?' Manju asked curiously.

'Oh, leave it, Manju. This thing will be out of our house soon, I promise you, Amma. And remember, Manju and Babu, you're not to speak of this to anyone.'

'As if we would,' Manju said angrily, her eyes flashing.

It's hard being young, Babu thought. People seemed to imagine you were idiots just because you were younger than they were.

'Your Appa won't be happy about this,' Amma said, not angry any more, only sorry.

'Appa? He's going to be out of it all,' Mohan declared. 'Don't forget he's going to be arrested today.'

A cloud came over Amma's face. 'I know. I hope there won't be any violence. I know you think Appa is wrong in tamely going to jail, Mohan, but try to think that there's a kind of heroism in that too. You don't always need revolvers and weapons to be brave.'

Babu and Manju realized how true this was that evening. The meeting was to be held on the maidan in front of the Post Office, the usual place for such meetings. But a little later two men came in hurriedly and said something to Amma. After they had gone, Amma said, 'I think you children better stay at home today.'

Manju, who had been watching her cat lap up its milk from a saucer, looked up in surprise. 'Why Amma?'

Being the youngest, Manju was always suspicious of being left behind. Mohan was almost an adult, and Babu was, after all, a boy; she was not only too young, but a girl as well. To which her reply always was, 'So what?' And nobody ever had a sensible answer to that.

'The meeting has been prohibited,' Amma said. 'And so they've decided to have it in the Market Square.'

Market Square was called Wilson Square after a British governor, but both Appa and Amma refused to call it that.

It was really a junction of five roads. There were shops on either side of three of the roads and in the centre of the Square was a sheltered rostrum for a policeman to stand on.

'You know how small and crowded that place is. If there's any trouble—and how can there not be, with the meeting being prohibited and the people in this mood—I don't want you both in it. You'll stay at home, won't you?' Amma seemed to be pleading with them.

'I want to come,' Manju said, putting on her stubborn look; but Babu, who had been thinking it over, said, 'We could go upstairs to Vivek's studio, Amma. We can see everything from there.'

Vivek was one of Appa's old students and had a photographer's studio on the first floor of a corner building—a splendid place from which to watch everything. Amma's face showed relief and Manju knew there was no danger of her being left behind. She flashed Babu a grateful look.

Vivek was alone in his studio and sprang up eagerly on seeing them. He slapped Babu heartily on the back and greeted Amma respectfully.

'Closing up?' Amma asked, seeing the closed windows.

'Vivek, can we watch from here?'

'Watch what?' Vivek tried to look blank.

'The meeting.'

'Who told you there's going to be a meeting?'

Amma laughed. 'Oh, they know everything. And they also know their father is going to speak.'

'Is he? Somebody said he's already been arrested.'

'He's going to be arrested now,' Manju announced proudly.

Vivek looked questioningly at Amma.

'That's right. We expect they'll arrest him now.'

'Vivek, can we stay here and watch?'

'Of course. I'll close the door so that we won't have any customers. You can have a good view from this window.'

While Amma talked to Vivek, and Manju went round admiring the photographs of newly-weds and babies, Babu stared out of the window.

It looked like any ordinary day, except that there seemed to be more people about than usual. The shops were full of customers and in the tiny triangle of a garden outside the Municipal Office, there seemed to be quite a number of people sitting and relaxing. The only unusual thing was that there were fewer vegetable sellers than usual. The tongas were there, however, waiting for customers, the horses placidly munching hay, the drivers snoozing on the back seats. As Babu hung out of the window, the usual peculiar combination of smells came to him—water sprinkled on dusty streets, flowers, rotten vegetables and horse dung. Where was Appa, Babu wondered. And where were the police? There were none now, but Babu knew how they could suddenly appear from nowhere.

Even as Babu watched, a small crowd was collecting in the middle of the road. Heads suddenly appeared on balconies, on roofs, above shops. The men lounging in the garden got up, and now, there it was, Babu saw with quickening excitement—the flag suddenly appeared above the policeman's shelter. And then the cry of 'Vande Mataram', 'Bharat Mata ki jai', 'Mahatma Gandhi ki jai'. How many people there were now! Amma, Vivek and Manju came running to the window, Manju shoving Babu aside, saying, 'Let me see, oh, let me see.' A man had climbed up on the policeman's stand and had begun speaking. Babu knew it was Damodar, a young Congressman. He was speaking in loud ringing tones, telling them about the arrests of the leaders, following on the Quit India resolution. And he spoke to them of the Mahatma's words: 'We shall either free India or die in the attempt; we shall not live to see the perpetration of slavery.'

The thick crowd around Damodar listened quietly, but there was some disturbance on the fringes. Policemen! Damodar, in one quick movement, jumped off the stand and was lost to sight. Someone else stood in his place.

'Look Amma, look Babu, it's Appa!' Manju's voice was shrill with excitement. 'It's Appa!'

How calm and composed he seemed! He stood there as if he was taking a Maths class in school. There were shouts and scuffles at the edge of the crowd. Perhaps the people were preventing the police from coming closer. Appa was speaking, but the disturbance prevented them from hearing his words. People near him were listening in rapt attention. And surely, Appa could not have made a joke at such a moment? But why then were the people laughing heartily as if they were enjoying one? They could see Appa's gestures, hear a few words now and then, but that was about all. It was maddening!

Now the crowds were being forcibly parted by the police. Lathis again and cracks and groans once more. Amma drew in her breath sharply, Vivek groaned once as if *he* had been hurt.

Appa's voice suddenly came loud and clear. 'Let them come. Don't fight back. Don't resist. But remember, the fight must go on.'

Two policemen were closing in on him and they soon seized him. Even as they held him, he shouted, 'Mahatma Gandhi ki jai.' The crowd shouted it back. And Babu felt that Appa looked straight at them and made a gesture with his head as both arms were held by the police. Then they took him away.

Manju began to cry quietly, shaking all over. Amma and Vivek took her away from the window. When she was quieter, she said, 'I wanted to talk to him. Oh, I wanted to talk to him.'

'Shut up, Manju,' Babu said roughly. 'Don't be a coward and a cry-baby.'

'I'm not,' Manju flared up.

'Appa wouldn't like us to cry,' Babu said.

'She knows that.' Vivek patted Manju comfortingly. 'She won't cry again.'

They went home feeling immensely gloomy. But Amma, as if determined to be cheerful, said, 'Come on now, let's eat something. I'm sure you're hungry.'

So they were. Babu's stomach was rumbling and he cheered up at the thought of food. Manju went into the backyard calling out for the cat. But of course, it refused to respond—it came only when it felt like it. In a little while the thump of Amma's hands beating out the rotis came from the kitchen and soon the wonderful aroma filled the house. Manju and Babu took their plates and sat impatiently in front of Amma, watching the sparks fly up from the wood fire. And then, there was a knock at the door.

'Babu,' Amma, her hands all floury, looked anxiously at them. 'Find out who it is before opening the door.'

'Amma, it's me, Mohan,' they heard.

It was Mohan with a girl. 'Amma, this is Suman,' Mohan said, bringing her straight in. 'She's doing her B.A. in our college.'

'Mohan, were you there? Did you see Appa?'

Mohan's face changed. 'Yes, I did,' he said shortly.

'Wasn't he brave, Mohan?' Manju asked, her face shining.

'Of course, he was. I mean, he is. I never said he wasn't. Anyway,' he looked at Amma's face and changed the subject. 'Amma, can you do something for us?'

'What is it?'

'Well, it's this speech of the Mahatma's. We want to translate it and make as many copies of it as possible so that it can reach everyone. Dinkar-kaka was to do it, but they arrested him. Suman is going to do the translation. Can you help her?'

'Of course.' Amma's face brightened.

'And another thing,' Suman spoke for the first time. Her voice was very soft. 'Can we bring a cyclostyling machine here? Tomorrow? We want to make lots of copies, quickly.'

'We have to finish the translation today. Here, Babu,' Mohan said briskly and curtly, 'Manju and you can go to bed. At once.'

'I'm not going,' Babu said simply.

'Now, listen,' Mohan began with a frown.

'I'm hungry. I'm not going until I have had my food.'

Mohan laughed heartily, shedding his air of authority. 'Sorry kids, I didn't know we interrupted your dinner. Well, we'll all have dinner in that case. I'm hungry too. And so, I'm sure, is Suman. Can you feed all of us, Amma?'

'What a question! Manju, get me some more flour.'

It was a surprisingly gay meal, though Appa was never far from their minds. Manju suddenly asked Mohan, 'Mohan, will they give Appa good food in jail?'

'The best,' Mohan said emphatically. 'After all, Appa is now His Majesty's guest. Go on, eat your food.'

After dinner Amma and Suman sat down to work. Babu and Manju watched them for a while, then went to bed. And listening to the low murmur of Amma's and Suman's voices as they worked, Babu understood what Appa had meant when he said, 'The fight must go on.'

IV

MANJU WOKE UP to the usual early morning sounds—the swishing sounds of someone washing a doorstep, the gurgling sounds of someone gargling, the chirp chirp of birds and the whirr whirr of Appa's charkha. Appa always started the day with some spinning. Manju listened idly to these sounds, feeling, as she always did when she heard them, that everything was all right. And then, suddenly, she remembered that Appa had been arrested the day before. He was not at home and it would be a long time before she woke up to the sound of Appa spinning. But then, if it wasn't Appa—who could it be?

Frightened, Manju rushed out of the room. It was Amma spinning, sitting under the window to get the early morning light. 'Amma?' Manju asked in astonishment. 'Why are you spinning today?'

Amma could never spin regularly like Appa did. Sometimes, when she was in the mood, she would sit at the charkha for hours. Or else, she forgot about it for days together. Now Amma gave Manju a wan smile. 'I thought I'd try Appa's way of beginning a day,' she said.

Mohan's head popped in through the door that led to the back passage. 'She wants to surprise Appa by spinning enough to make a shirt for him,' he said solemnly, spoiling it the next instant by giving Manju a huge grin.

Amma, without stopping or looking up, retorted, 'No, this one is going to be for you.'

Mohan, unlike Amma or Appa, wore clothes made out of mill cloth. 'What has independence to do with wearing hand-spun clothes and all that rot?' he would ask Appa impatiently. 'First, let's drive out the British. That should have top priority. All other things come next.'

'This spinning programme is more important than you imagine, Mohan,' Appa would explain. 'Unless we can provide work for ourselves, what use is independence?'

'Okay Amma,' Mohan said now, 'it's a deal. You spin enough for a shirt and I'll wear it.'

'Amma,' Babu complained later, 'are you trying to give Mohan his shirt all in one day?'

Amma laughed. She had been sitting there for more than two hours now. Meanwhile Manju, under Amma's directions, had brought in the milk, boiled it, swept and cleaned the kitchen. Babu had had his bath and was waiting for breakfast, while Mohan, whistling softly between his teeth, cleaned his bike.

'I'll get up now. Ooooh, I'm stiff. Oh, my poor legs.'

'Don't forget my shirt, Amma,' Mohan's voice came from the back passage. 'You can't get off by moaning about your legs.'

'You'll get your shirt, young man. Now children, give me one hour and I'll have your meal ready. I have to go out myself after that.'

While the food was cooking, Amma plaited Manju's hair into one long, neat plait. Babu had joined Mohan in the bike cleaning and Manju could hear a continuous buzz of conversation from the two of them. Soon after lunch, Mohan went off to college and Amma, after clearing up, went out too. She said she would be back in a hour.

Manju had just settled down with a book when she was startled by Babu's urgent hiss, almost in her ear. 'Manju, I say, Manju.'

Manju looked up from her book with a start. 'Oh Babu, what is it? How you startled me!'

'Listen, I'm going out. Want to come with me?'

'Where?'

'I'll tell you later. If you want to come, just say so and come quickly.'

'But Amma?'

'We'll lock the house and leave the keys with Ramabai. We'll be home before Amma anyway. Are you coming? If not, I'm off.'

Manju jumped up in a flurry. 'I'm coming. Wait for me.'

Babu was waiting with the huge lock and key when Manju came out. He locked the door, gave the lock a tug to make sure it was locked, then thrust the key at Manju. 'Go and give that to Ramabai.'

Manju held back. 'I'm not going. You go and give it.'

Ramabai, their nearest neighbour, was a prying, inquisitive woman. She had to know everything. Her questions were endless and came so fast that Mohan had nicknamed her 'A question-a-second-Ramabai'.

'Don't be silly. You're just wasting time. Hurry up now.'

'I don't like to go to her. She keeps asking questions.'

'So what? Just shut her up.'

'Why don't you shut her up?' Manju asked suspiciously. 'Are you scared of her?'

'Me? Scared of her? Ha ha! You're the one who seems to be scared of a snoopy old woman. And then you want to take part in the movement. Girls!'

Manju glared at him, snatched the key and said, 'I'll be back in a second.'

'Time for one question anyway,' Babu grinned.

'Please give this to Amma when she returns. Babu and I are going out but we'll be back soon,' Manju gabbled, all in one breath and turned away before Ramabai could utter a word. She thought she had got away when Ramabai yelled, 'Hey, Manju, where are you going? Only Babu and you? Does your mother know? Where has she gone? Where's Mohan?'

'Don't know. Back soon,' Manju called back over her shoulder and fled.

'Now,' she asked Babu impatiently, 'tell me where we're going.'

'To watch a procession. Walk fast. We may be late.'

'What procession? Whose procession? Where?'

'You sound just like Ramabai,' Babu said. 'Did she give you a quick lesson?'

'Oh, shut up about Ramabai. Tell me, Babu. What procession? Don't be so mean.' Manju struggled to keep up with Babu's longer strides.

'The college students are taking out a procession from their college to the Collector's office. Mohan told me we could watch. He says it's going to be peaceful.'

There were already some people lining the roads. Manju and Babu found a good spot, almost opposite the gate of the Collector's compound. They had to wait for sometime. In a while, it began to rain. It had been drizzling off and on since the morning. But this was a heavy downpour—the usual monsoon rain, heavy and steady. People rushed for shelter. Manju and Babu sheltered themselves under a large tamarind tree.

'Look at me!' Manju exclaimed. Her hair was plastered to her head, her clothes clung to her, a large drop hung on the tip of her nose. She giggled at herself, but Babu, after a guffaw, said guiltily, 'Why don't you go home and change?' Manju refused.

Soon they heard the magical words: 'They're coming, they're coming.' The children, like the others, rushed out, heedless of the rain. Policemen now appeared all along the road. Some of them walked in front of the students, some by their sides; but the students marched as if the police didn't exist. They walked in complete silence. There were no slogans, no shouts, just the shuffle of feet, the drip drip of rain and a low murmur from the watching crowd.

Babu and Manju looked eagerly for Mohan. Yes, there he was, dressed in white pyjamas and a cream-coloured shirt, with another boy, both holding aloft a picture of the Mahatma. Their arms must have ached holding it up that way for so long, but their faces were expressionless.

Now the leaders of the procession—Suman was one of them, they saw in excitement—had reached the barred gates. A police officer—he was the D.S.P., Mohan told them later—came up to them. There was some conversation between him and the students. The students seemed to be arguing. The rain had lessened now and the police officer took off his hat and ruffled his hair. Once he laughed, showing all his teeth, but the students remained serious. Now one of them handed him a piece of paper. He took it without glancing at it and nodded.

The students turned their backs on him and one of them shouted, 'Mahatma Gandhi ki jai.'

'Jai!' the others shouted back loudly. And then they briskly marched back the way they had come.

'Is that all?' Manju asked in disappointment.

'What else did you want? A dance? A drama?' Babu asked scornfully. Nevertheless, he understood her feeling and asked Mohan the same question when he returned home. 'Why did you go back so quietly? Were you scared of what the police would do?'

Mohan seemed immensely pleased with himself. 'Scared? Not by a long chalk. We had planned it this way. We knew they would stop us at the gates. We knew they expected us to protest and be violent. Oh yes, they wanted us to do that so that they could beat us up, haul us away to jail. But we are not prepared to go to jail. Not as yet, not until we've given them much more trouble. And so we decided we would give them no chance at all.'

'What was the point then?' Babu asked, while Manju listened earnestly, her chin cupped in her hands.

'It's like a declaration of war. We've told them now—this is war, and for us, you're the enemy. You don't start a war without first declaring your intentions, do you?'

'Unless you're Adolf Hitler,' Amma, who had been quietly listening to them, said with a small smile.

'Right. Which we're not. So, that's how it was.'

'And what was that paper you gave the policeman?'

'That was a notice we served on the Collector, as a representative of His Majesty's government, asking them to quit India or else face the consequences.'

Suman and another boy turned up after they had finished their dinner that night. The boy staggered in with a large newspaper-covered parcel in his hands.

'Got it?' Mohan asked, his voice tense with excitement.

'Yes. Lot of trouble, though. Where shall I take it?'

'Here, let me help you. My room okay, Amma?'

'No, I think the puja room is better. A light there will look more normal.'

'Right as usual, Amma. The puja room, then.'

The boy went away after a whispered conversation with Suman. Then Suman, Amma and Mohan went into the small puja room. Babu and Manju stared curiously over their shoulders at the mysterious parcel which turned out to be a cyclostyling machine.

'Babu,' Mohan said as they settled down to work, 'sit out in the front room and keep a watch. Give us a warning if anyone seems to be coming to our house. Manju, go to bed. Or else,' he went on, noticing her crestfallen face, 'you sit here in the hall and pass on Babu's warning to us.'

Amma, Suman and Mohan got down to work at once. They worked in the dim light of the oil lamp that burned before the gods. Manju peered at them from the hall. In a little while, she began to feel drowsy, and had to struggle not to doze off.

Babu sat outside, alert and attentive. He felt a thickening in his throat. It was beginning. And at last he was doing something. What a pity Gopya, Murali and the others would never know about it. Perhaps, some day . . . . He checked himself and kept his eyes and mind on the road outside. It was deserted. In a little while the nine o'clock siren went off. Babu thought for the first time that day of the war being fought all over the world. And suddenly,

coming out of his reverie, he tensed. A man riding a bike got off and stopped right outside their gate. But it was only to light a cigarette, it seemed. Babu could see the match flaring, then the glow in front of the man's face. The small point of light moved as the man got on his bike and rode away. One more bike. Yes, this man was getting off. Maybe he too—no, he was opening their gate. Babu flung himself inside. Manju turned a startled face to him.

'Someone's coming in.'

There was silence. From inside the puja room, three faces looked at him blankly, the dim light giving them a peculiar look. Shadows quivered and danced as the wick in the oil lamp flickered and fizzed. Then Amma got up and came out, followed by Mohan. Suman stayed inside and Mohan closed the door of the room.

'Manju, to bed. Babu, you too.'

There was a knock at the door. Babu rushed to his room, unrolled his bed roll and threw himself on it.

A knock again.

'Who's there?' Amma called out.

Knock knock.

'Mohan, go and see who it is.'

Manju, who had got into her bed too, noticed that though Amma's voice was steady, her hands trembled.

Mohan came in saying, 'Amma, it's Patil, the Sub-Inspector.'

Amma held Manju's hand in a tight, hurtful clutch, though her voice was still cool and calm. 'What does he want?'

'He wants to talk to you.'

'To me?'

The hand relaxed. Manju drew her own hand back and rubbed it softly.

'I haven't come to trouble you,' a strange voice said. 'Your husband was my friend in school. I'm a friend.'

Amma got up quickly and went out. Manju waited a

moment and followed her. There was Babu coming out of his room, making a show of having been woken out of a deep sleep. Rubbing his eyes, yawning loudly and repeatedly, mumbling in a grumpy voice, 'Who is it? Who is it?' But nobody paid him any attention and soon Babu was taking in everything with the greatest curiosity.

The man—was he really a police officer? He didn't look like one in his dingy clothes—was saying to Amma, 'Yes, we were in school together. Oh, he was far above me. He was a scholar and I was one of the dunces. He always helped me, though. God knows how often I would have been caned, but for him.'

'Please, Patil saheb,' Amma said rather impatiently, 'tell me why you are here.'

'It's like this.' Suddenly the man was brisk and business-like. His glance swept over all of them, taking them all in shrewdly. Certainly, this man was no dunce. 'There's going to be a search in your house.'

'When?'

'Most probably tonight. I heard the Sahebs talking. They were speaking of a cyclostyling machine. It seems you people are making copies of the Mahatma's speech. They say you have people hiding here as well.'

'Ha!' Mohan scoffed.

'But you have the cyclostyling machine?'

'No,' Mohan said instantly.

'Have you?' the man asked Amma.

'No,' Mohan repeated angrily. 'You're wasting your time spying on us.'

'Tell me,' the man ignored Mohan and spoke to Amma.

'Yes,' Amma replied simply and Mohan made an angry hissing sound.

'Where is it?'

'Amma, you've gone . . .'

'Inside.'

Manju's heart began beating wildly. Why was Amma giving them away?

'Give it to me. I'll get it out of the way. You can have it when it's safe.'

Mohan burst out again, 'Amma, what are you doing? How can you trust a policeman?'

The man touched Mohan on the shoulder. 'Mohan, you're still very young. There are many things you don't understand. I am a policeman, yes, but your father was and still is my friend. And this is my country as much as it is yours. Now, give it to me quickly. They may come any moment.'

Amma opened the door of the puja room and said, 'Suman!'

Suman emerged, wiping her face with her sari, looking anxiously at them.

'Come in,' Amma beckoned to the man. 'It's here.'

Suman stared at Amma and the man in bewilderment. Amma smiled at her and said, 'You've got to get away, Suman. Take away all that material. Mohan, will you . . .'

Mohan stared at Amma, at Suman, and finally at Patil, who stared steadily back at Mohan. And suddenly the two smiled at each other.

'Okay, Amma,' Mohan said and ducked into the puja room. He lugged the machine out and gave it to Patil.

'Do you have a largish bag with you?' the man asked.

'Manju . . .' Amma began but Babu had already got it.

'That's fine, that's fine,' the man said.

And then they were gone—Patil, Mohan and Suman. The house seemed unbelievably quiet after the earlier intense activity.

'Let's go back to bed,' Amma suggested.

Mohan came back shortly. 'Suman?' Manju asked him anxiously.

'She's all right.'

'Go to bed, Manju,' Amma said.

Bed? With the police about to come? It was impossible. But nevertheless, she did drop off at some time. And came out of her sleep with a jerk to hear a loud knock at the door. It was repeated. Manju sat up in sudden fright. Amma patted her comfortingly. 'Who is it?' she asked loudly.

'Open the door,' a strange voice ordered.

'Mohan, see who it is,' Amma said.

It was like going through something all over again. But this time they knew for sure it wasn't a friend standing out there. No need for Mohan to announce: 'Amma, it's the police.'

V

FOR LONG AFTER, even when they were grown up, Babu and Manju remembered that night. It was like a nightmare, all those huge, burly figures filling up their small, tidy house. The electricity had, as it often did, failed, and there was only a kerosene lantern on the floor to provide some light. It threw strange, wavering shadows on the walls. The policemen's shadows were grotesque and gigantic, reaching up to the ceiling, making the house seem even more crowded than it really was. There were also, adding to the illusion of a crowd in the house, the harsh sounds of the policemen's footwear on the stone floor.

'They walked in with their shoes on,' Amma complained bitterly, the one time, the only time, she spoke of it later. 'They didn't spare even the puja room and the kitchen.'

There were ugly scraping, screeching sounds as the men pulled out trunks, and loud clangs as they let the lids fall down carelessly when they had done searching inside.

There was a small black trunk in which Manju kept her treasures—coloured pictures, two old wooden dolls, a tiny silver purse and a collection of shells that Manju had gathered when they had gone the year before on a holiday to Karwar. The policemen opened this trunk too, and after going through its contents, contemptuously dropped the shells all over the floor. As they walked about, the delicate shells cracked and crunched under their feet—tiny, crackling sounds that hurt Manju more than anything else. She had been standing quietly until then, as still as Amma, Mohan and Babu. Now, as the shells crunched into bits, she made a sudden movement and a horrified sound. And then she felt Amma's hand, which had been quietly resting on her shoulder, press down as if restraining or comforting her. Manju looked up questioningly, but Amma's face was stony. There was no expression on it.

And then they were gone, angry in their disappointment that they had found nothing, hateful in their anger, leaving behind them a dirty, littered home, and four persons savage with anger. And silence.

It was Amma who came out of it first. 'Come on, all of you,' she said, her voice as flat and expressionless as her face had been earlier. 'Let's clear up.'

They set to work in silence. Amma, in spite of the late hour, even washed the floor as if she wanted to wipe out all traces of those hateful feet. And Mohan, who usually grumbled about Amma's 'cleanliness' helped her without a word. At last they were done, and unrolling their mattresses, they tried to get to sleep. It had been a long day—was it only yesterday that Appa had been arrested?—and they were tired. Yet, Babu found himself awake. And he guessed from the restless movements that came from Mohan's bed that Mohan couldn't sleep either.

A little later Amma called out, 'Mohan?'

'Yes, Amma?'

'Awake?'

'Yes.'

Amma came in. 'Mohan, I've been thinking. Who knew that you would bring the cyclostyling machine here today?'

'Why, Amma?'

'Well, how did the police come to know? They were very definite about it. Someone must have told them.'

Mohan whistled through his teeth. 'Of course! You're right.'

'How many people knew about it?'

'There's Bhausaheb, Mukund, Suman. Maybe Shiva, and one or two others. I don't know who else, Amma.'

'You know what this means. There's a traitor somewhere.'

There was a soft thud as if Mohan had hit something—his pillow, maybe. 'Traitors, traitors. God, always traitors. That's how we lost our country. Will we lose it again?'

A little later, when Amma had gone back to bed, Babu heard Mohan mutter to himself, 'I must warn Sadanand.'

'Mohan,' Babu said in a soft whisper.

'What?' Mohan's voice was distant, as if he was thinking of something else.

'Where's Sadanand?'

Suddenly Mohan turned on Babu fiercely. 'Listen Babu, don't ask such questions. It's better you know nothing. Don't even mention the name Sadanand again. Understand? Will you remember?'

There was silence after that, except once when Mohan said in an angry and bitter voice, 'Traitors!'

Traitors—the word was a seed that had been planted that night, and it sprouted in Mohan's college three days later.

Manju and Babu had gone to Bhat Master's house that morning. Amma, worried about their studies with school closed indefinitely, had had a talk with Bhat Master—a master in their school and a good friend of Appa's. The result was an arrangement for them to go to Bhat Master's house every day for lessons in Science and Maths. Mohan and Amma would help them with the other subjects. Though they grumbled about it, the children found it a relief to have something definite to do each day. And then, they soon realized, having lessons in someone's house was not like having them in a school. Bhat Master's wife popped in and out to give him his tea or paan-supari; the youngest kid, a toddler, staggered in sometimes, making them laugh at his antics. All these distractions provided relief from the monotony of lessons; on the whole, it wasn't bad at all.

That morning they were returning home after lessons, when they met Murali. He stopped abruptly at the sight of them with books in their hands. He stared in blank astonishment for a moment, then asked, 'Have you joined the government school?'

'Don't be an idiot,' Babu said angrily.

'What's this, then?'

'Lessons—with Bhat Master,' Babu said shortly.

Murali immediately made a sympathetic face and said, clicking his tongue rapidly in mock sympathy, 'Tch, tch, tch, poor boy. That's what happens when you're a Master's son. Poor child, poor child.' And he patted Babu consolingly on the back.

Babu jerked away irritably. 'Oh, stop that, you fool. Where are you going?'

'To college.'

Manju's jaw dropped. 'You mean you've joined college?'

'What else!' Murali said solemnly. 'They invited me, they wouldn't take a refusal, they insisted, so . . . .'

'Murali, you're a fool. Where are you going?'

'I told you. College.' And then, winking at Manju, 'I have to give Satya's medical certificate to the college office.' Satya was Murali's elder brother. 'Satya has typhoid and my father's scared they'll strike his name off the register if he's absent. They may think he's gone and joined Gandhi. And what will my father do then? He wants a son who's an M.A., LL.B. He has no hopes in me at all. Coming with me?' he asked Babu.

'Sure. Manju, you go home. Here take my books.'

The moment they came in sight of the college building, it was obvious something was happening. The students should have been in their classes. Instead, they seemed to be everywhere—in the corridors, the porch, on the grounds. Babu and Murali dutifully made their way to the college office first. They gave the certificate to a bored looking clerk, and at that moment a bell rang.

'What's that for? What's happening? Why is everyone out?' Murali eagerly asked the man.

The clerk, dipping his pen in an ancient-looking bottle of ink—Babu noted with fascination that a spider had spun a web between that and the edge of the table—shrugged his shoulders without even looking up. He went on with his work, ignoring them. Murali made a face at Babu over the man's head, imitating the man's shrug. Babu grinned.

They came out into the corridor to find the students moving in a steady stream—all of them in the same direction. Babu saw a friend of Mohan's among them. It was Iqbal, a tall, serious-looking boy who could imitate people marvellously well.

'Iqbal, Iqbal,' Babu called out. Iqbal heard his name, looked around, saw Babu and held up his hand as if to say 'Wait'. In a moment he was with them.

'What are you doing here, Babu?'

'Iqbal, what's going on?'

The two questions came out almost simultaneously.

'The principal is giving a talk to the whole college.' Iqbal made a comical face.

'I say, Iqbal, come on, man, hurry up,' a voice said.

'Coming. Look, Babu, you better go home. Mohan won't like your being here.'

'Why?'

Iqbal bent down, suddenly dropping his voice.

'We're expecting fireworks. Going to be lots of bangs, I believe.'

He left them and soon the corridor was deserted except for the two boys. Someone in the office was typing and the clackety clack of the typewriter was the only sound now.

'Well,' Murali said reluctantly, 'let's go home.'

'Why not,' Babu paused and went on hesitantly, 'why not go for the lecture? You heard what Iqbal said. Fireworks. That means . . .'

'Trouble!' Murali's eyes were dancing with excitement. 'Come on, let's go and have a look.'

When they approached the hall, they could hear the Principal's voice. The talk had already begun. The

Principal was speaking in a slow, pompous manner, stopping frequently to emphasize something. The hall was overflowing. Students stood at the back, all along the wall, they stood in the aisle between the seats, in clusters at all the three doors, and many of them peered in through the windows. Babu and Murali, by a process of wriggling, reached one of the windows and looked in.

The Principal was on the dais, walking up and down, taking jerky turns each time he reached the end of it. He was gesticulating wildly. 'You are all students, remember. Students. Not agitators or revolutionaries. Though some of you seem to think that's what you are. I know who these fellows are. I have my eye on them. Take care, don't be led away by them, don't be misled. There are traitors in your midst . . . .'

'Yes, there are traitors,' a voice shouted back.

'Who said that? Stand up. Stand up.'

Silence.

The Principal glared at everyone in the hall, and went on. 'As I was saying, there are traitors among you. Stay away from them. Report their names and activities if you come to know of them. Expose them as the traitors they are . . . .'

'Traitor yourself,' said a voice, quivering with anger. A girl's voice. Babu found it faintly familiar. 'Traitor to your own country.'

'Who said that? Who said that?' The Principal almost danced around, trying to find out where the voice was coming from. But now there was pandemonium—so many shouting voices, so much noise, that nothing of what the Principal said could be heard. He looked ridiculous, his mouth opening and closing, his eyes almost popping out of his head, trying vainly to make himself heard above the din.

Suddenly a figure dashed onto the stage. It was Suman, Babu saw in excitement. Her lively, round face was alight with emotion and as she began to speak, the noise died down. The Principal, Babu noticed, was held down by two boys who wouldn't let him speak.

'Friends,' Suman's clear voice rang through the hall, 'I'll tell you who the traitors are. They're those who think of themselves, their jobs, their comforts, instead of their country. Those who lick our rulers, yes, lick their boots just to keep their precious jobs and live in comfort. This government has put our leaders in jail, they've throttled us, gagged us, they're putting out the light of freedom. Will we allow them to get away with it?'

'No, no, no,' the cry rang out loud, bouncing back from the walls.

'Join us, let us unite and drive out these foreigners. Wake up, all of you. Swaraj is not far. Swaraj is near, if we all unite. What can even the whole British Empire do against a country determined to throw them out?'

'Police, police,' some voices called out agitatedly.

The Principal, who had relaxed, began to struggle again.

'Give up your studies, refuse to cooperate with the government in every way. Act like the citizens of a free country. We will not obey the laws of tyrants.'

'Police, police.'

'Wake up, don't be cowards. Act like brave and free men and women. Act now.'

'Police . . . .'

There was a tumult near the doors. Students surged backwards and forwards. 'Suman, get out fast!' someone yelled. Suman, and the two boys who had held the Principal, jumped down. Babu and Murali found themselves pushed aside as boys began jumping out of the windows. There were groans, cries and shouts from inside the hall. Some students were racing down the corridor. Babu and Murali joined them. Shrill police whistles sounded everywhere. As the boys came out of the building, they heard a cry of: 'The flag, the flag.' A few students were staring up at the roof.

A police officer, followed closely by two constables, pounded up the iron staircase, making a tremendous drumming sound.

'Let's get out,' Murali panted.

'We can't go that way,' Babu said, noticing the police vans parked near the main gate. 'Let's go the other way.'

They raced through the gardens, over a low wall, and they were out. Babu looked back once—the flag was fluttering on the roof. Murali and Babu parted with scarcely a word.

Babu went home thinking of Mohan. Had he been there too?

'Of course he was,' Amma said when he told her and Manju all about it. 'He was one of those who were to hoist the flag.'

'Do you think the police could have got him?' Manju asked, her eyes apprehensive.

'I hope not. We'll just have to wait and see.'

Mohan didn't return home. It was the police who came to them in the evening. 'We have a warrant for his arrest,' they said. Babu saw the relief on Amma's face. This meant they hadn't got him as yet.

One of the policemen tried to bully Amma into telling him where Mohan could be. Her steady 'I don't knows' seemed to make him furious. Amma, however, showed nothing—neither fear nor anger.

Finally the police went away, looking rather shamefaced. And Babu thought that Amma was right. They've arrested Appa, they're going to arrest Mohan, they've put Gandhi in jail along with so many others, they have beaten up boys and girls. But as long as we're not scared of them, it's all right.

A little later however, Amma broke down. She buried her face in her sari and began to sob as if she would never stop. Babu and Manju looked at each other aghast. If Amma broke down, what would they do?

'Amma, please,' Manju said, putting her hand on Amma's back. Babu said nothing, just gruffly cleared his throat and stared at the wall.

Finally, Amma looked up, and wiping her face angrily and roughly with her sari, said, 'What a foolish thing to do!'

Babu sighed in relief. And Amma said, with a small smile, 'We're going to manage, aren't we?'

'Of course,' they said emphatically.

Yes, they would!

VI

THEY KNEW THE police were keeping a watch on their house, waiting for Mohan to return. He did not come, though, nor was there any news of him. Though this was, in one way, a relief, it didn't help not knowing where he was or what was happening to him. But it was not just them now. It was everyone, in every part of the country. Their fears for Mohan, their worry about Appa—these became part of a much greater thing as they realized the same thing was happening everywhere.

'It's as if a sleeping tiger has been awakened,' Amma said when they were discussing these happenings with some visitors.

Hartals, processions, meetings, demonstrations—students came out of schools and colleges, people gave up government jobs, they burnt foreign clothes, and changed over to the Gandhi cap. It was as if everyone was standing up and shouting: 'We are free. We will not be ruled by you any more!'

Soon, things that would have been unbelievable, impossible a few days earlier, became commonplace and routine. For them, their town, it began with the burning of the railway station. Babu woke up that night to find Amma shaking him, saying, 'Babu, get up, get up.'

He was wide awake in a moment. 'What is it, Amma?'

'Come out and look.'

They went into the veranda. Manju, standing on a chair, was looking through the grille. No need to ask what she was looking at, no need for Amma to point it out to him. Babu could see it clearly himself. Flames leaping up high—the whole sky had turned an angry red colour.

'It's the station, the railway station,' said Amma.

'It's burning,' Babu said stupidly, as if he had made some discovery.

After that they watched in silence. Occasionally huge billows of smoke went up. The choking, acrid smell of it came to them with the wind. In a while, the flames leapt up again and now they burnt steadily. And then, there was nothing at all but a dark sky and pale columns of grey smoke. Later, Babu realized that the most frightening thing about it had been the silence, the absolute silence. There had been no sounds at all, not even the usual nightly sounds of dogs barking.

The next morning they heard all about it. Not just one, but four railway stations had been burnt, almost simultaneously, as if the operation had been planned. Their station, they heard, had been burnt to cinders. No one went there, not even to see how it looked. Two boys who had gone there out of curiosity early in the morning, had been arrested and charged with having taken part in the burning. The police seemed desperate to lay their hands on anyone.

In Bhat Master's house that morning there was an excited babble of sounds, instead of the usual sedate questions. No one wanted to start lessons.

'That's enough now,' Bhat Master said when he decided they had chattered enough. 'Open your books.'

During lessons Babu could feel Bhat Master's eyes rest on him every now and then. Babu felt very uneasy. What was it? What had he done?

When lessons were over, and the boys got up, Bhat Master said to Babu, 'Wait, Babu, I have a book of yours with me. I'll just get it.'

'My book?' Babu was puzzled. 'Which one?'

But something in Bhat Master's face silenced his questions. Babu waited patiently. All the boys left. Manju, who had finished her lessons earlier, was playing outside. Then Bhat Master came out and deftly pulling away one of

Babu's notebooks from under his arm, slipped something in between the pages. 'Give this to your mother,' he said. 'No, no, don't take it out now. Go straight home and give it to your mother. And listen, tell her if she has something to give in return, to send it with you tomorrow. Put it in a book and give me the book. Okay?'

Babu felt dazed and could only just nod.

'All right, then. You can go.'

Babu went out, his head in a whirl. Manju came running up to him and walked beside him chattering, but Babu heard nothing. His head was full of questions.

Amma was waiting for them, reading the newspaper.

'Amma,' Babu said urgently.

'What? Hungry, are you?'

To her surprise, Babu, ignoring her words, went into the hall, pulled something out of a book and gave it to her. 'Bhat Master asked me to give this to you.'

She took the paper from him, opened it and said, 'My God!'

Manju, on her way to the bathroom, stopped at that. There was something even more curious—Amma was smiling. How rare that was these days!

'My God, it's from Mohan.'

'Mohan!'

Babu and Manju rushed to Amma and peered over her shoulder. They read the letter together.

To Amma, Manju and Babu—my greetings.

I am sorry I had to go away without meeting you.
I hope, Amma, you were not worried.
I am well—don't worry about me at all. I will try to
get in touch with you from time to time, whenever
it's possible. But, if you don't hear from me, don't
get anxious. It's better for you not to know where

I am. Babu, don't get into any trouble. Help
Amma all you can—both Manju and you. Don't
tell Appa about me if you have a chance to send
him a message. I am perfectly well and happy.
Look after yourselves.

Yours,
Mohan

'Well!' Amma exclaimed with a smile.

Babu snatched the letter from her and read it all over
again. Then it was Manju's turn.

'Give it to me when you're done,' Amma said.

Manju thought she would read it and put it away.
Instead, Amma went into the kitchen with the letter. There
was a small lamp burning there. Amma dipped the letter
into the flame. The paper caught fire, blazed for a moment,
then died down, leaving nothing but charred bits.

'Thank God,' Amma said.

'Why did you burn it?' Manju asked, aghast.

'It's better this way,' Amma said briefly.

Babu then told Amma they could send a reply to Mohan
through Bhat Master. That night Amma wrote a small note,
Manju and Babu added their bits and Babu put the note in
his Maths book.

'My Maths book, sir,' Babu said gravely to Bhat Master
the next morning.

'All right.'

When Babu got the book back, the note had gone. Babu
and Manju wondered where their note would go now, how
many hands it would go through before it reached Mohan,
and where was Mohan?

Something happened that day, however, which drove
all thoughts of Mohan from their minds. That afternoon a
group of masked men attacked the post office, locked it
from the outside, and set fire to all the mail. They also cut

the telephone wires before they left. By the time the police arrived on the scene, they had fled.

Everyone talked about the incident. And suddenly the name Sadanand was on everyone's lips. It was Sadanand who was organizing these things, the people whispered. The police and government officers were getting panicky—because of Sadanand. The British government was on the run—Sadanand's work. Small boys and young people murmured his name admiringly, older people disapprovingly.

In their house not much was said. Amma's face looked even more anxious. Was Mohan involved in all this? After all, how long would he escape the police? And, where was he?

It seemed the police wanted the answer to this question as much as they did. It was the biggest blow they had been dealt so far when the children returned home from classes the next day and found no Amma at home. The door was bolted from the outside. Fearfully, they opened it and went in.

'Amma?' Babu called.

There was no reply. Manju looked into all the rooms. 'Amma?' she called out too, her voice shrill with a touch of panic in it. It was not like Amma to go out without letting them know.

'Maybe she's in Ramabai's house,' Babu suggested, though his face showed he didn't believe it. Amma wasn't one of those women who went about to gossip. 'Go and look, Manju.'

The next moment there were sounds of hasty footsteps in the backyard. 'Manju, Babu!'

It was Ramabai's youngest daughter, Maya. Manju flew to the door.

'Manju,' the girl looked strangely at Manju. 'Where's Babu? Oh, there you are. Your Amma . . . . '

'Where is she? Is she in your house?'

The girl—she was just a little younger than
Mohan—shook her head, and swallowed. Why was she so
nervous? What was it? Babu felt his skin prickling with fear.
Something seemed to clutch him, in so tight a grip, that he
could scarcely breathe.

'No, she's not with us.'

'Then, where is she?' Manju demanded angrily. How
could Amma go away like this?

'She . . .' the girl hesitated, then blurted it out bluntly.
'The police took her away.'

'No!' Manju cried out, her face crumpling. Babu looked
at Maya angrily. But Maya's sympathetic face told him it
was true. He felt blank and empty. Manju began to moan,
'Amma, Amma.'

Now Maya rushed forward, held Manju tightly by the
shoulders and said, 'Look, Manju, now, don't cry. You're
not to cry, or I won't tell you anything.' Maya was crying
herself. 'They haven't arrested her, I promise you they
haven't. Come inside, I'll tell you all about it.'

Babu, still dumb, followed them in. He felt blank.

'Listen,' Maya said, 'I was here in the morning with your
Amma when the police came. They wanted to know where
Mohananna was. They took your Amma away to question
her about it.' She saw Manju's terrified face and said, 'Now,
don't. She's all right. She told me to tell you that. Actually,
she was more worried about you two. I promised her you
would be all right, you wouldn't cry. Now, what will I say
to her if you behave this way?'

Babu who had been listening despairingly—Appa gone,
then Mohan, now Amma—not really taking it in properly,
asked Maya, 'She wasn't scared for herself at all?'

'No,' the girl said wonderingly. 'Not a bit. Just worried
about you. Specially Manju.'

'I'm all right,' Manju now declared, feeling a bit
ashamed of herself. Babu looked pleased and thankful.
Thank God, no tears. He just couldn't cope with tears. They

made him angry, that's all.

'That's good. And your food is ready. Come on, have a wash and have your lunch. I'll serve you both. I told Kaku I'd do that.'

They didn't really feel like eating, but when Maya told them it was she who had cooked lunch—Amma hadn't finished cooking when she had had to leave—they didn't have the heart to disappoint her by not eating. After lunch, the three of them cleared up. Maya and Manju then settled down to rangoli designs—both of them loved creating new designs—when they heard Ramabai call Maya.

Maya jumped up. 'There's Mother. I'll be back in a moment.'

When Maya returned, Babu could see she was angry, though she was trying to hide her anger. He guessed what it was. 'Maya,' he said, 'if your mother doesn't want you to be here, you go home. You don't have to get into trouble because of us.'

'What nonsense!' she scoffed. 'My mother doesn't understand. She thinks the police will arrest me because I'm here. Father knows I'm here, he asked me to stay until your mother returns and that's what I'm doing.'

They were lucky Maya was with them. It would have been dreadful to have been alone, staring at each other, thinking all the while of Amma and what could be happening to her. Maya didn't let them mope. She played with them, chatted, sent Babu out for a little shopping, made them help her in cooking some sort of a meal. But when the day came to an end, and darkness crept in, their hearts felt heavy and dismal. As if it wasn't gloomy enough, the electricity went off and they had to make do with the dim light of a lantern. One small tear came down Manju's face, then another, and finally it was a downpour. Maya silently comforted her. In a little while it was over.

'Go and wash,' Maya told her. 'You'll feel better.'

When she was splashing water on her face, there was a

knock at the door. Babu and Maya raced to the door and Manju, dropping the brass mug with a loud clang, followed.

But it wasn't Amma. It was Vivek. It was drizzling and his hair and face were wet. 'Is it true,' he asked, 'that they've taken your mother away?'

Vivek was the first of many visitors. Suddenly the news seemed to have spread and they came to them—friends, colleagues of Appa's, neighbours, all making anxious inquiries about Amma. Many of them tried to persuade the children to go home with them, but Babu and Manju were adamant. They would rather, much rather, stay right here at home, waiting for Amma. Maya was with them, wasn't she? Finally Vivek decided to stay the night just to keep them company.

Manju made Amma's bed before she made Maya's and her own. As she tried to sleep, she heard the murmur of voices from Babu's room. It was somehow soothing, as also were Maya's soft snores, and finally she dropped off to sleep.

It was terrible beginning a day without Amma. The children sat feeling lost and hopeless—Maya had gone home for a bath and change—until Babu determinedly shook Manju into doing some work. Maya was pleasantly surprised to see them cheerfully tackling the morning chores when she came back. She prepared breakfast while the children had their baths. They were clearing up when they heard the sound of the gate. Some more visitors, Babu thought, when they heard Amma's voice calling out, 'Manju! Babu!'

Manju, who had piled up the used plates before taking them into the backyard, dropped them and a terrific din followed. The next few minutes were completely chaotic. None of them knew what they said or did. Only after a while did Babu notice a man waiting outside. He made a low and respectful namaskar to Amma before leaving.

They went into the house and the children saw, with a

sense of shock, how exhausted Amma looked. She collapsed on the ground as if her legs could hold her up no longer.

'Amma, can I get you some water?' Babu asked.

'Kaku, there's hot water, have your bath,' Maya suggested.

Manju held on to Amma as if she was afraid she would be whisked away from them if she let go. Amma smiled wearily at all of them.

'Thank goodness you were here, Maya. I didn't worry about Manju because I knew you would be with her. As for Babu, I didn't worry about him at all.'

Babu, coming back with a glass of water, felt immensely proud when he heard that. 'I don't know what we'd have done without Maya when Manju went boo-hoo, boo-hoo,' he grinned.

'I didn't . . . I never . . . .' Manju began indignantly.

'Sorry, it was just a sniff-sniff then,' Babu corrected himself.

'Sssh,' Maya hushed them. 'Kaku, go and have your bath.'

After a bath and breakfast, Amma lay down and slept. Vivek came back a little later, then many others. But Amma slept on and the children didn't wake her. At first they hushed each other, saying, 'Sssh, Amma's sleeping.'

Then, Manju began to get scared. What if Amma was dead? She was so still, so silent. She went in every few minutes to reassure herself with the sight of Amma's chest moving up and down.

It was almost dark when Amma woke up. Manju had lit the lamp in the puja room at Maya's suggestion. And then Amma woke up and began to talk. She told them of her ordeal. Not all of it, though, Babu shrewdly guessed. But enough.

'They kept asking me about Mohan. They're sure it's Sadanand who's responsible for all these things that have happened—the burnt railway stations and all that. They

know Mohan is with him. They know so many things I'm surprised they don't know where Mohan is,' she said bitterly. 'They wanted me to tell them that. Just imagine! And they went on and on about Sadanand. I said I didn't even know who he was. They kept threatening that they would put me in jail and what would the two of you do in that case?' Her lips tightened, making her look an entirely different person.

'How little they know us! Did they imagine I would tell them anything because I was afraid for you? I knew you'd be all right; someone would look after you. I knew you'd be brave and that you wouldn't like me to do things I shouldn't out of fear for you. They knew—I wonder how—that Mohan had sent us a letter. They wanted to know who gave it to me.'

Manju thought of Mohan's letter smouldering in the fire. How glad she was now that Amma had burnt it!

'And then they said I had to get ready, they were going to take me away from there. I was sure they were taking me to jail. Instead they took me out of town to a traveller's bungalow. I don't know where it was. There was a big sitting room inside with all the saheb's type of furniture. And Appa was there, sitting on a hard, wooden chair.'

'Appa!' all three of them exclaimed. Then Babu asked, 'How is he, Amma?'

For the first time she smiled, though the smile stayed only in her eyes. 'He's shaved off his moustache. "One thing less to look after," he told me. Without it, he somehow looks younger. They told him: "Here's your wife. Tell her to cooperate with us. Or else, she'll go to jail and your two children will be on the streets." They left us alone, but we knew they would listen to our talk. Appa and I didn't even mention Mohan's name. He asked me about the two of you, and about your studies. And he told me he was well—lots of good company in jail, he said, even better than outside—and that we were not to worry about him. And then the Inspector came and asked us, "Well?" And Appa said, "Well?" And I said, "I know nothing!" And Appa smiled at me.

'They took me away from there, brought me back here, left me in the police station the whole night, all alone. In the morning they said—it was the D.S.P. himself, I believe—the D.S.P. said, "We're sorry for all the trouble." And I said, "What trouble?" And they said, "You can go now." I came out and there were people waiting for me and I came home.'

Later that night they had another visitor. It was Sub-Inspector Patil.

'Call him in,' Amma said.

He sat cross-legged in silence for a while, then asked Amma, 'Are you all right?'

She nodded, giving him a small smile.

'Do you trust me now? Will you listen to me?'

She nodded again.

Now he leaned forward, both his face and voice urgent and earnest. 'Go away. Go away from here. Take the children and go.'

'Why?' Amma asked after a pause that seemed to last forever.

'They're going to give you a bad time. Our Saheb has gone mad. Have you heard? They've removed sleepers from railway tracks, and trains can't run. They've taken away revenue collections from vans, mail from post offices. They're attacking everything—railway stations, post offices, police stations. It's not just one tree now, or a few trees—the whole forest has caught fire. And the sahebs have gone mad. They've made your son a proclaimed offender. They're hoping to get at him through you. They think if they harass you sufficiently, he'll give himself up. And through him they are hoping to get that other person—you-know-who. I won't mention names. It's *him* they're really after. They want to go, get hold of him and hang him.'

Babu went cold. Hang him—he knew who the 'him' was, it was Sadanand. But Amma was listening quietly, her eyes fixed watchfully on Patil's face. 'How will my going away help?'

'If you're not within their immediate reach, they may forget all about you, see? After all, they're not going to chase you, I'm sure. They'll start on someone else. So just take the children and go. Go to friends, relations, anyone. Go to a small place, preferably—you'll be safer there. Don't stay here now. Not even for a day.'

VII

WHOEVER SAID A village was a quiet and peaceful place? Babu and Manju, after only a few days in the village, certainly didn't agree. The racket began early, when it was still dark, with the crowing of the cocks. There was one persistent cock somewhere nearby, who started off with a harsh, challenging cry. Getting no reply to his challenge, he would repeat the call, going on and on, making sure that they couldn't go back to sleep. Besides this, there were the deep, lowing sounds of the cattle which were—how strange it seemed at first—nearly next door. There was only a roofless, sunken courtyard separating the open pillared hall—where the children slept—from the cattleshed. If ever they woke up at night, they could hear the restless rustlings of the cattle among the straw. And early mornings, as they lay in bed, awake, but too lazy to get out, there would be all those waking-up noises. Sounds of people gargling, spitting, hawking and coughing. Loud voices in conversation. Then, the jingle jingle of cattle going to the fields, and the scraping sound of a wooden plough being dragged behind.

Cattle and cowdung—you just couldn't get away from these. The smell of cowdung was everywhere, for the cowdung itself was everywhere. It was used in the kitchen each morning to plaster the floor and fireplace, it was diluted with water and sprayed by hand, in a neat circle, just outside the front door to provide a base for a rangoli design, a different one each morning. And on the roads too, the smell followed you everywhere, for the cattle placidly dropped large dollops of dung as they walked.

For Manju the village meant flies ever after. Flies that came in swarms—fat, contented, lethargic flies that you'd have thought could easily be killed. But no, when one settled on Manju's arm and she swatted at it vigorously, all that she could do was to hurt herself, while the fly lazily moved to another spot and settled down there.

'You don't hit hard enough,' Babu advised her. 'Here, I'll show you how to do it.'

'No, thanks,' Manju said, refusing the helpful offer, for Babu had a wicked glint in his eyes. 'I can manage my own flies.'

'You can't!'

Amma, listening to the two of them, smiled. They were back to normal now, bickering and squabbling as usual. She was glad she had listened to Patil's advice—and almost everyone had agreed with him—and got away. At first, she had been reluctant. Where would she go? Appa's parents were both dead, and she didn't feel it was right to go to either of his sisters. Her own father was dead, too, and her mother stayed with her brother, a government officer, and Amma couldn't go there! It would have got him into trouble.

And then, providentially it seemed, Annu-kaka turned up. He was no relation, really, just a great friend of Amma's father. He was a formidable figure, specially to the children, with his enormous height—his turban made him look even taller—and his stern face on which no smile dared show itself. But, Amma always said, he had a very kind heart and a soft corner for Amma and her children. There had been a time, they knew, when he had been in trouble, and Amma's father had helped him out. He never forgot that.

'Come with me,' he said as soon as he heard about Appa and Mohan, and about Amma's own ordeal. 'You can't stay here alone. And it isn't as if the children have school. Come to us and we'll somehow manage some lessons for them. Vanmala's kids are there, you know.'

'But, Annu-kaka,' Amma looked at him with a troubled face, 'you know how it is with us. There's Mohan—he may want to get in touch with me. And we don't have a good reputation with the police right now. You may get into trouble because of us. And then,' she smiled, 'you know you don't approve of our ideas.'

Babu remembered that Annu-kaka always had arguments with Appa about the freedom movement. 'It's none of my business,' he would say when Appa urged him to take part in it. 'I've got my work, my lands, and what's the use of wearing a Gandhi cap and shouting "Mahatma Gandhi ki jai" and going to jail? Far better if each one does his own work—the country will take care of itself.'

Now, however, he didn't say a word against Appa and Mohan, or what they had done. 'That's all your business, Sonu,' he said. Sonu had been Amma's name before marriage. 'I won't interfere with you and you don't interfere with me. And forget about getting me into trouble. That's my problem and my worry. I certainly won't leave you alone here at such a time.'

And so here they were in Narayanpur—Annu-kaka's place. Vasant, Annu-kaka's grandson, got furious if Babu and Manju called it a village.

'It's not a village,' he would protest. 'It's a town.'

'It's not,' Manju would reply instantly. 'It's a village.'

Both Manju and Vasant could go on forever with one of these 'it is', 'it isn't' arguments. They never seemed to get bored with it. Amma however, found it intensely irritating and boring and ended the argument one day by saying, 'Well, if you compare Narayanpur to Bombay, Calcutta, London, New York—I suppose, it is a village.'

'There!' Manju shot out triumphantly. 'What did I tell you!'

'But,' Amma went on, ignoring Manju, 'if you compare it to Sannur,' this was the tiny village where most of Annu-kaka's lands lay, 'it's a town.'

'There!' Vasant grinned. 'What did I tell you!'

Town or village, the children enjoyed being there. Manju loved Annu-kaka's house. The huge front door, studded with shining brass knobs, fascinated her. In addition, there was a very high threshold, with a brass strip across it, and a door frame which had colourful designs painted on it. Above the door hung a festoon of brass mango leaves, with a portly Ganapati in a small niche above. You entered the house through the cattleshed which was dark and mysterious, with eyes shining and gleaming out of the darkness, wet tongues licking you and tiny heads butting you. Most of the rooms in the house had wooden pillars spiked with nails. On these nails were hung all kinds of things—shirts, coats, turbans, dhotis twisted into knots, saris, mirrors and even necklaces. It was, Manju privately thought, the best way of putting away things. Reach for a nail and there you were!

At first the change felt good; it was nice, too, to be fussed over by Annu-kaka's wife whom they called Ajji, and his daughter, Vanamala-auntie, who was widowed and lived with her parents. For company they had her two children—Vasant, who was a little older than Manju, and Shanti, who was only eight. But Vasant and Shanti had their school—Vasant went to the government school in the next town and Shanti to the Narayanpur school—and Manju and Babu began to find Narayanpur dull. There had been so much excitement recently, that life felt very tame. Annu-kaka had promised Amma he would 'see about lessons' for them, but in the meantime they had absolutely nothing to do.

Babu had lost no time in telling Vasant about their recent activities—specially about Appa's and Mohan's exploits—and Vasant chafed at having nothing like this to do.

'If only,' he would say, his eyes going all dreamy, 'if only I could join Mohan! Next time you send him a message will you ask him if they'll have me? Promise me you'll ask him.'

'But Annu-kaka won't allow you to do that, will he?'

'Oh, Ajja! I can manage him,' Vasant said grandly, waving his hand airily as if his grandfather—of whom he was, as a matter of fact, terrified—was a mere nothing.

'How?' Shanti asked bluntly and plainly. 'When Ajja calls out "Vasant" in that voice of his, I've seen you shiver,' she said. And Manju and Babu burst into laughter at the expression on Vasant's face.

He yelled at Shanti, 'And who said you could poke your nose into our talk? Go and play with your dolls. Or your pots and pans. Shoo now.'

'Who are you to shoo me?' Shanti, who was an independent little girl, asked. 'And just because I'm a girl, it doesn't mean I must always play with pots and pans. Sonu-auntie says it's wrong to talk that way. Look at what's her name, Manju?'

'What's whose name?'

'That woman who helps Gandhi and writes poems?'

'Sarojini Naidu,' Manju said, smiling at the description.

'Yes, Sarojini Naidu. Look at her.'

'I can't see her.' Vasant, who could act the fool very well when he wanted to, shaded his eyes with his hand and pretended to search. 'Where is she?'

'What she can do, I can also do.' Shanti, who had a single track mind, went on, ignoring Vasant's antics.

'Well, go and write a poem then.'

'And what will you do?' she asked challengingly.

'I'll go out and join the struggle and throw the British out and make our country free.'

'Hurrah!' Babu shouted enthusiastically, throwing his cap in the air. And then, catching it neatly, he said in a more subdued manner, 'But we won't ever get a chance here. It's too quiet. Nothing ever happens.'

That very evening, however, there was some excitement. Annu-kaka was frowning over some accounts when a servant came in and said, 'The Sannur police-patil wants to see you.'

Annu-kaka went out. Soon it seemed as if a dozen men were arguing outside. The children went out to see what it was all about and found that there was just one man, talking at the top of his voice. The man's size was a complete contrast to his voice—even Babu was taller than him—and he had a peculiar habit of flinging his arms about as he spoke.

'Who do they think I am?' he was saying. '"Go and get them," he tells me. As if they're waiting for me to go and get them. "It's your responsibility," he says. Why mine? Just because it happened in Sannur? It's true it happened there, but what I say is—where are the men who did it? Not in Sannur! No, certainly not there! Tell me, who in Sannur has the courage to touch Government property when I'm around? It must be someone in this place, Narayanpur, who's done it. And it's his responsibility in that case, isn't it, not mine?'

'Well,' Annu-kaka interrupted him irritably, 'what do you want me to do?'

'It's like this, Sahukar Annappa.' Suddenly the man dropped his aggressive manner and spoke ingratiatingly. 'You see, the thing was done on your land. One of the poles had fallen in one of your fields. Perhaps your men have seen something. I tried to ask them, but they looked at me as if they were buffaloes. They pretended they knew nothing. But if you, Sahukar,' he folded his hands and spoke in a pleading tone, 'ask them, they'll tell you everything. I'll never forget this obligation all my life. Until I find out something, that Sub-Inspector is going to make my life miserable. Help me, Sahukar.'

'I'll see what I can do about it,' Annu-kaka said curtly, immediately adding, 'You can go now.'

The man lingered, but Annu-kaka walked out and he had to leave. The children, left alone there, looked at one another in amazement. What had it all been about?

'Let's go out and ask that patil chap,' Vasant suggested. 'He only wants a chance to yap yap anyway. Once, when there was no one he could talk to, he was found talking to a tree.'

'I don't believe it,' Manju replied instantly.

'Ask anyone if you think I'm lying. Ask my mother.'

'And in the meantime, the police-patil will get away,' Babu said impatiently. At which point they rushed out hastily.

The police-patil was ready to leave, one leg flung over his bike, one still on the ground. Seeing them he got off and it was nearly half an hour before he got on again. By which time the children knew in full detail what had happened. The telegraph wires had been cut in Sannur and the Sub-Inspector had told the police-patil to arrest the men responsible.

'What does he think, eh, that the men are still there, waiting for me to go and arrest them, eh?' He chuckled at his own wit and then went on more seriously. 'I know one of the men who must have been in it. He's got to be involved in this thing.'

'Who?' three voices asked.

'Aaaaaaah!' What a sound that was! 'That's a question which won't get an answer that easily. Just you wait and see the fun. He'll be sorry he ever insulted me,' he said mysteriously and chuckling again at something, he rode off.

'I wonder who he means,' Vasant said, chewing his lips thoughtfully.

'No point in playing guessing games,' Babu replied indifferently.

'But Babu, if we know the person and . . . .' And suddenly Vasant clicked his fingers in a series of triumphant clicks. 'I know. I KNOW.' His whole face was shining with triumph. He looked expectantly at the others, obviously waiting for the question which promptly came.

'Who?'

'It's Bhima. Bhima of the gymnasium.'

Babu knew the man he meant. There were very few people, if there were any at all, who didn't know him. Bhima was not his real name. What it was, perhaps everyone, including Bhima himself, had forgotten now. He became Bhima when he was a child because of his size and enormous strength. Now he ran a gymnasium where young men came to wrestle, and younger boys for body building.

'This patil had a quarrel with Bhima once. I don't remember why, but the patil is supposed to have gone to Bhima's gymnasium to complain. And Bhima didn't say a word. He just picked the patil up as if he were a sack of onions or something, carried him all the way to the end of the lane, dumped him there without a word, and calmly walked away.'

Manju and Babu laughed heartily, now understanding why the patil had chuckled so gleefully at the thought of getting Bhima into trouble.

'Let's go and warn Bhima,' Manju said impetuously.

'Now? Not a chance! Almost dinner time now and I wouldn't like to give Ajja a reply when he asks us where we have been.'

Suddenly, there was Annu-kaka's voice asking, 'And what are you all doing here?'

Vasant nearly jumped out of his skin, biting his tongue so hard that tears came into his eyes. 'Nothing, Ajja, nothing,' he stammered. 'Just . . .eh . . . uh . . . talking.'

'Well, stop talking and come and have your dinner.'

It was Ajji who gave them a chance to get out after dinner. 'Oh God!' she suddenly exclaimed. 'I quite forgot.' She banged her palm against her forehead, her habitual gesture, for she was always forgetting things. 'Gangabai asked me for some milk and I told her I'd send some through Timma. Has Timma gone or is he still here? Go and find out, children.'

Timma had left. 'Ajji,' Babu said, trying to keep the

eagerness out of his voice, 'we can go and give the milk to Gangabai if you want.'

'Will you?' she asked gratefully. 'Take it at once. The poor woman will be waiting. What will she think of me?'

'What but that you forgot as usual.' Vasant grinned at her.

'Vasya,' his mother said mechanically.

'What did I say?' he asked innocently.

They delivered the milk first, then, on the way back, went to Bhima's gymnasium. Even now there were some activities going on. They could hear the grunts of two men trying out some wrestling holds, while Bhima stood poised over them, calling out instructions. An oil lamp glowed before the large picture of Hanuman while a man was getting dressed in a dimly lit corner.

'Hey, Bhima,' Vasant called out from the door.

Bhima came to them immediately, a genial giant, rumpling Babu's hair, playfully pretending to wrestle with Vasant.

'I say, Bhima . . . stop it, stop it, I say. I want to tell you something.'

'What is it? Are you challenging me to a fight? I give up, man. I can't possibly fight you.'

'Huh, don't try to be funny. I'm serious. Honest! The police-patil, our Sannur police-patil, is going to have you arrested.'

'What!'

'Yes,' Vasant nodded, pleased with the effect of his words. 'He thinks you cut the telegraph wires, you know, near Ajja's lands in Sannur, and he's gone to tell the Sub-Inspector about it.'

'Arrest *me*?' It came out as a magnificent, offended roar. 'He! That punk is going to arrest *me*?'

'What for?' A quiet voice asked.

Bhima, his face looking as if he was going to explode, turned to the man who had spoken, the one who had been dressing in a corner, and said, 'Have you heard his cheek, his impudence, that pygmy, that dwarf, that matchstick, that drumstick . . . .'

The children spluttered and shook with helpless laughter.

' . . . daring to get *me* arrested?'

'I asked you—what for?'

'Cutting the telephone wires, I believe. I cut the telegraph wires! Am I a monkey to climb up a telegraph pole and cut the wires?'

'Listen Bhima,' the young man said irritably, 'will you just stop speaking for a moment and let me talk to these children? Now, children . . . .' He gave Babu and Manju a keen look and then shot out at them, 'Are you Jagannath Rao's children?'

'Yes.'

'I see.'

He looked at them thoughtfully. Babu wondered what he was thinking. He was a thin young man—a few years older than Mohan—with a careless expression on his face. He had a slim pencil line of a moustache and short hair. He was smarter and better dressed than most of the young men in the village.

'Mohan's sister and brother too, aren't you?'

Again they said, 'Yes.'

There was something in his voice that made them proud of being related to Appa and Mohan.

'And what are your names?' he asked them. They told him. For the first time he smiled. He had a very attractive smile.

'I'm Arvind,' he introduced himself. 'Okay, now tell me what all this is about poor Bhima.' Bhima began muttering angrily again. 'Please, Bhima, don't talk, not yet. Tell me what's all this about his being arrested.'

Vasant, who had felt left out and ignored all this while, launched into an explanation before Babu or Manju could say a word. Arvind listened patiently, not interrupting, and then said, 'Good! You did the right thing by coming here to warn Bhima. Lucky I was here. You can go home now with easy minds.'

As they turned to leave, Babu had an odd feeling that there was something more the man wanted to say. And he was right. They had scarcely taken a few steps when they heard him call out, 'Babu!' Babu went to him immediately.

'Look, Babu,' Arvind sounded awkward and nervous, 'I know I shouldn't ask you this—maybe, I'm wrong, I really don't know.'

'Is there something you want me to do?'

Arvind looked at him for a moment without speaking, then said, 'Yes, but not so that you get into trouble. Your family has had more than its share of that.'

'Tell me what it is,' Babu pleaded.

'You don't have to do it if there's any risk involved.'

'Okay.'

'Right then. It's this. Keep your ears open and let me know if there's anything—anything at all which you think I should know. You know what I mean?'

Babu nodded.

'You understand what I'm saying?'

'Yes.'

'That's fine. Off you go.'

'What did he want?' Manju and Vasant wanted to know.

'Who is he?' Babu asked in his turn, stalling for time.

'He's Arvind,' Vasant said, as if that explained everything.

'Idiot! As if I don't know that!'

'He's the Vakil's brother. He's studying Law in Bombay.'

'Oh!'

'He should be there now, actually. I don't know why he's here at this time.'

Babu knew. Arvind had come for a purpose. And Babu knew too, what that purpose was. Babu had imagined that there was nothing going on here. Now he knew he was wrong. Here too, the tiger was waking up. Babu was thinking this over when Vasant said, 'Now, you tell me what he said to you.'

Vasant was such a blabber mouth. Could he keep anything to himself? Babu thought not. Manju, well . . . she'd never speak to anyone, he could trust her. But Vasant . . . .

'He said . . . .' Now what could he say to put off Vasant? ' . . . not to tell Annu-kaka about our coming to warn Bhima.'

'As if we would!' Vasant said, scornfully.

Manju, however, knowing Babu better, knew there was something more. She raised her eyebrows and asked Babu a question silently. Later, Babu signalled. Later.

VIII

THE EXCITEMENT OVER the telegraph wires soon subsided. Bhima was not arrested as there were plenty of people to vouch for his innocence. In fact, the police-patil was severely reprimanded for leading the police on a false trail.

'I knew,' Vasant grinned, 'he would make an ass of himself. He always does that.'

They soon realized that this was but one of many other happenings. A young man who had just returned from Bangalore told an interested audience about events taking place elsewhere. The railway station closest to them, about twenty-five miles away, had been burnt down just a few days back. Everywhere fish-plates had been removed, and railway lines so disturbed that trains could not run. People who did travel on trains did so now without tickets. 'Why should we pay money to a government which is not ours?' they said. There were some appreciative chuckles and clucks at this.

But Annu-kaka, when he heard of this, was disapproving. 'This isn't the right way,' he said. 'Today they are doing it to this government, tomorrow they will do it to our own government. Who will stop them then?'

But Babu who, with Vasant, had listened to the young man, wondered—would these people never do anything themselves? Would they just sit and listen to stories of what others were doing? Surely, young men like Arvind wanted to do something? Surely, they would *do* something? And if they had any plans, Babu wanted to be in it with them—if they would have him, that is.

They ran into Arvind the next day, Babu almost literally so. Vasant and he were going towards the market when they saw Arvind. When Babu saw who the other person was with Arvind, he gasped, and would have called out the name if Arvind, banging into him, hadn't suddenly steadied him saying, 'Ah, careful now, careful. Look where you're going, boy. Are you hurt? No? That's all right then.'

And, even before Babu could indignantly deny that he had tripped, fallen, banged into Arvind (on the contrary, it had been Arvind who had banged into him!) or anything else, Arvind and his companion were nearly fifty paces away. And now Babu recollected who Arvind's companion was. It was Mukund, Mukund who had brought the cyclostyling machine to their house that day. And now he knew this too—Arvind had tried to prevent Babu from blurting out Mukund's name. Mukund had looked quite different too, with a moustache and long hair. Perhaps he was in disguise. Which meant—and Babu's face brightened at the thought—that Arvind was planning something. Perhaps something would happen at last.

Yet nothing happened and there was, instead, just the same old routine. To make matters worse, Amma had fixed up an old master to give Babu and Manju some lessons. He was a horrid old bore who did nothing but drone, eyes closed, a wad of tobacco held in his mouth, so that one cheek bulged. And suddenly, when Babu was trying hard not to doze and Manju, with a bored face, was doodling away, drawing faces, the old man would open his eyes and break out, 'Understood? Understood?' And then, not waiting for their reply, he would expertly spit out of the window, a stream of red liquid that fell with a plop into the yard outside.

'I'm not going to him,' Babu would say mutinously each day. 'The old bore knows nothing, nothing at all. He knows even less than Manju and I do.'

'Only for a while, Babu,' Amma pleaded. 'Until we find someone else. You know Annu-kaka is on the look out.'

'What about Arvind?' Annu-kaka suggested when Amma asked him for the hundredth time if he'd found someone.

'Arvind who?' Amma asked.

'He's the Vakil's youngest brother. A clever boy, but doesn't seem to work hard. A pity. He was doing law in Bombay and now, for some reason, he's come home and is whiling his time away. Dresses like a dandy, too,' Annu-kaka snorted. 'The Vakil was telling me he wished the fellow would do something, anything, rather than just mooning about. He may welcome the idea, though whether Arvind will . . . .' Annu-kaka raised his huge shoulders in a massive, disapproving shrug.

But Arvind, to Annu-kaka's surprise, agreed to the suggestion. The children gratefully stopped going to the old master. And now they had a pleasant surprise as well. Arvind, they realized, was not only better than the old bore, he was really good. He could teach Science better than even Bhat Master could, which was surprising, considering the fact that he was a law student.

'This is what I wanted to do, really,' he told Babu and Manju with a wry smile. 'But my brother insisted I study law so that I could help him with his practice. Well,' he shrugged, looking careless and casual once more.

Arvind, unlike any other teacher they had known, treated them like friends. He put on no airs, and he didn't seem so much to teach as to share exciting information. They rarely stuck to the boundaries of lessons, but talked of many things, specially the war which was now going on. Arvind was very sure that Russia would be the end of Hitler. 'And I tell you, Babu and Manju,' he said with the utmost earnestness, 'however much we may dislike the British for what they're doing to us, I can only hope they defeat Hitler. I can't imagine the state of the world if they don't. But somehow, I'm sure they will. If only the Russians give the Germans a good fight . . . .'

The one subject they never discussed, strangely enough, was their own freedom struggle. Babu and Manju, who had decided to ask him about Mukund, found that Arvind could cleverly evade questions when he wanted to.

'By the way,' Arvind said one day when they were leaving, 'I won't be home tomorrow. Come a little early the day after. We'll try and make up for the lost time.'

That day Vasant came home unexpectedly early from school. 'They let us off,' he said, adding cheerfully, 'there was a robbery in the school, I believe.'

'Robbery? What could they rob from your school?' his mother asked sharply, wondering whether Vasant was making up a story to get away from school. 'And who got hurt?'

'Hurt? No one,' Vasant said rather sadly.

'Then it isn't a robbery,' Amma said laughing.

'Isn't it?' Vasant asked innocently. 'Anyway, they took all the papers from the Headmaster's office, files and registers and things like that. And they burnt them right there in the courtyard. I saw the ashes,' he boasted as if he had done something remarkable. And then, wistfully again, 'I wish they'd burnt the whole school.'

'Vasya!' his mother said angrily while Babu laughed.

'What did I say that's wrong?' Vasant asked, making a face. 'After all, it's a government school, isn't it? I don't like attending a government school. Gandhiji says it's wrong. Look at Babu and Manju. They don't go to a government school! Why can't I go with them to Arvind's? Why can't I?' he asked challengingly.

'Don't ask me,' his mother said calmly. 'Ask your Ajja.'

'I will. I'm going to ask him,' Vasant said, thrusting his hands in his pockets and striding up and down. 'It's not fair. There's our great leader, Mahatma Gandhi, telling us not to go to government schools. Why should I?'

'Why don't you ask your Ajja these things? Why ask me?' his mother said irritably this time.

'I will,' Vasant said again. 'I'm not scared of him,' he bragged. When they began to laugh, he glared at them and said angrily, 'See if I don't.'

'But,' his mother went on placidly, 'before you go and scare your grandfather, do me a favour. Since you're home, you may as well make yourself useful. Go to Sannur, Babu and you, and tell Sangya that your Ajja wants him to . . .' and she gave them a list of instructions.

'I'm going with them,' Manju said quickly when the boys got ready, caps on heads, slippers on feet.

'No, you can't,' Amma said. 'It's four miles there and four miles back. Too much for you.'

'But, Amma . . .'

'I said no. You can't do it.'

The boys had already gulped down their food, but to Babu's surprise, just as they were leaving, Ajji gave them a small snack to eat when they reached Sannur. 'Are we spending the day there?' he asked in surprise. Vasant grinned and said, 'Just you wait and see.' He knew from experience how hungry a four-mile walk could make you, specially when you knew you had another four-mile walk ahead of you.

By the time they reached Sannur, it was midday. Vasant and Babu found Sangya—Annu-kaka's oldest and most trusted servant—sitting with the other workers in the shade of a tamarind tree and having lunch. 'Lunch' was rotis tied up in an old cloth, some kind of dry, cooked pulses rolled up in them, with onions and chillies to munch for relish. The cattle were resting too, munching, chewing, their huge jaws moving, their eyes dreamily closed, their bells sounding suddenly and musically as they moved to whisk flies off their bodies.

'Aha,' Sangya beamed at them, 'there you are, Vasantappa. Now, what are you doing here at this time?

What happened to school? Nothing left for you to learn, eh? Or have your teachers got fed up with you at long last and thrown you out?'

They were old friends, Vasant and Sangya, and this chaffing was a normal routine. After explaining their errand, Vasant and Babu sat down to have their own snack. Babu, whose mouth had begun watering at the sight of the workers' food, now understood why Ajji had given them a snack. 'Bless her,' he said as they tucked their feet under them and opened the brass container.

'Go in and eat, boys, go in and eat,' Sangya urged them.

'In' was an old house in which Annu-kaka's father had lived. Now it was just four walls and part of a roof. Annu-kaka used it as a place in which to camp when he had to stay on in Sannur during harvest time. There was a small blackened fireplace in one corner for cooking and a well outside for water.

But Babu and Vasant had already begun eating, Vasant saying to Babu, 'There, didn't I tell you we'd be hungry?'

'Hungry?' Babu retorted. 'I'm starving.'

Sangya, who had finished eating, went away to drink water, wash and gargle. He came back, wiping his hands on the end of his turban. And then, like a magician, he pulled something out of his turban, and looking conspiratorially around, said to the boys in a whisper, 'Boys, can you read this out to us?'

'What is it, Sangya?' Vasant asked curiously. 'Is it a letter? Who's been writing to you, you old rascal?'

But Babu had seen instantly what it was that Sangya held out and he exclaimed, 'That! Where did you get that?'

'Why do you want to know?' Sangya asked in his turn, looking at Babu rather suspiciously.

'Because . . . because . . .'

'Because my mother helped to translate that and we made copies of it in our house,' Babu wanted to say. For he had seen that the paper held by Sangya was a copy of

Gandhiji's speech. But Babu didn't complete his sentence. 'Give it to me,' he said instead. 'I'll read it out to you.'

The men listened seriously, their eyes fixed on Babu's face. Vasant watched in admiration as Babu stopped at difficult words and explained them. After he had finished reading, he told them how, after this, Gandhiji and so many leaders had been arrested, and how the government had been so scared of what the people might do in their anger, that it had all been done in the greatest secrecy. And also how so many more who protested when the news spread, had also been put into jail. 'My father too,' Babu said simply, and tongues clicked sympathetically. But, Babu went on, there were many who hadn't done anything at all, and yet they had been arrested too. Sangya, to show his whole-hearted sympathy and disapproval, nodded so vigorously that his turban fell off, revealing a bald head, as round as a dome. One little boy who had brought his father's lunch and had been listening open-mouthed, not understanding a word, sniggered at the sight. Sangya, giving him an angry glare, hastily put his turban back on his head, while the boy's father absent-mindedly cuffed the boy on his head, saying, 'What are you braying like an ass for?'

And then, Babu had no more to say, and Sangya put out his hand and took the paper from him, putting it back carefully in its place, inside his turban.

'Who gave you that?' Vasant asked curiously, repeating Babu's earlier question.

'I found it somewhere,' Sangya replied and there was something sly in his face as he spoke. But a moment later he got up saying, 'Back to work, fellows,' and he seemed to be the same old Sangya after all.

Vasant and Babu strolled around, ending up in the old house. Sangya peeped in and said, 'I thought you two had gone.'

'No, we're going in a moment. I say, Sangya, who's been

cooking here?' Vasant asked, pointing to the fireplace which showed distinct signs of having been used very recently.

'Cooking?' There was a flash of something—fear or anger, Babu could not exactly make out—before Sangya put on a look of ignorance. 'Why, it's your Ajja.'

'But Ajja hasn't stayed here for ages. Months. Why, I came with him the last time myself. This looks as if someone has been cooking here regularly.'

Sangya gave a laugh which sounded both feeble and false to Babu. 'Regularly, eh? Who should cook regularly here? Don't I sleep here myself with Raja?'

Raja was the stringy dog who lay lazily near the well the whole day, getting up occasionally to move away from the sun.

'And doesn't Raja bark even if he hears a mouse?' Sangya went on rather belligerently, as if Vasant had accused him of something.

'Something odd about Sangya,' Vasant said when they started off for home.

'Odd,' Babu said thoughtfully. 'Yes, he's hiding something.'

'But Babu,' Vasant protested, 'Sangya is the most honest fellow ever. He'd never tell us lies. Ajja knows he can trust him completely.'

'Even then,' Babu began, but left it at that. There were many other less controversial things to talk about.

The way back seemed much longer, perhaps because they were a little tired. But even though his legs had slowed down, Babu's mind was clicking away. First Mukund, then Arvind, now these pamphlets and Sangya's strange behaviour. Surely, taken together, they showed something. Surely it indicated that there was some activity going on underground which would soon surface?

When at last they reached the main street of Narayanpur, it was obvious that here there was some unusual activity going on. A large police van with barred windows stood in front of the Treasury—the place where the government money was kept. Two armed men stood near the open door of the van and two others at the Treasury entrance. A man now staggered out of the door carrying something in his hands, and with him, on either side, were two more armed men. Babu and Vasant stopped and watched curiously.

'Money,' Vasant hissed in Babu's ear.

There was the usual number of idlers sitting on the compound wall of the Treasury office, and a few others loitering inside the compound. Nobody seemed to be very interested in what was going on. It was all very peaceful and normal. In fact, the boys never knew how it all began, but all at once, there was chaos.

A terrific number of bangs sounded simultaneously and smoke swirled about. The boys could see the armed men dashing about, but suddenly there were so many men round the van, that nothing could be clearly seen. Babu noticed one man, the loose end of his turban drawn round the lower half of his face, struggling with another— struggling, Babu realized, for the rifle. More bangs, a loud crack, a scream . . . .

Babu and Vasant instinctively ran to the compound wall, looking for cover, yet unable to tear themselves away from the scene. It was impossible to take in all of what was happening. The boys saw and remembered only bits and pieces which fell into place later, giving them a clearer picture: a man rolling on the ground as if in agony; another pulling off his slippers and hurling them at someone; a struggle near the door of the van. As the smoke slowly cleared—the bangs, the boys found out later, had been only crackers—they noticed that many of the men were masked, their faces, except for their eyes, hidden. Apart from one or two groans, one startled scream and one muffled cry, as if someone was in pain, there was total silence.

And then, as suddenly as it had begun, it was over. There was a flurry of activity as the men began to run in all directions. Some of them passed close to Babu and Vasant, who were by this time, crouching near the wall. And Babu heard one man say, 'Scatter now. Fast.'

'You're hurt,' another voice said.

'Go now. Don't waste time,' the first voice said.

And then they were all gone. There was complete silence. The boys got up and looked at each other. And then, for the first time, all around. Not a person was on the roads. The doors of the houses opposite the office had been bolted from the outside. A few people who, like them, had been watching, began to move quietly. One of them muttered to them, 'Get away from here quickly.' The boys noticed a few figures, trussed up, lying near the van.

It was only the next day that they knew what had really happened. It had been a raid on the revenue collection from a number of villages. The amount—more than Rs 7,000, it was said—was being taken away, when the men had attacked. They had got away with both the money and with the rifles.

'The strangest thing is,' Annu-kaka told them the next day, 'they rarely keep all the money here. This time they must have hoped this would be a safe place. We haven't had any trouble here—not so far.'

'Who do you think those men were?' Ajji asked idly. 'Not our Narayanpur people, I'm sure.'

'Why?' Annu-kaka asked ironically. 'Are your Narayanpur people different in any way?'

'They wouldn't take part in a robbery, would they?'

'Look at Babu,' Annu-kaka said with a smile. 'He wouldn't like it to be called a robbery, would he? I'm sure he has something to say about it.'

But, oddly enough, Babu had nothing to say. He was absorbed in his own thoughts. Who were they? The question seemed to be on everyone's lips. Babu, however, thought he had the answer to that one. He had recognized one of the voices as the men made their escape. A voice that had taken him back to a night at home—Appa and the others talking, the moonlight coming in through the window and himself lying on Mohan's bed. He had heard this same voice that night too. And he knew whose it was. It was Sadanand's. Sadanand here? Did that mean Mohan was near them too? Had Mohan been one of the masked men last night?

Babu's excitement, which he couldn't share with anyone, almost threatened to choke him.

IX

VASANT HAD BEEN so overcome by what he had seen that
he went to bed in total silence. His mother was so worried
by this that she went over to him and felt his forehead with
the back of her hand. 'Have you got fever or something?'
she asked anxiously, while Vasant squirmed
uncomfortably.

The next morning however, much to her relief, he was
back to normal. He took advantage of Annu-kaka's and his
mother's preoccupation with other matters by tagging on
to Manju and Babu when they went to Arvind's, instead of
going to his own school.

'Don't you have to go to school?' Manju asked
suspiciously.

'No,' Vasant said casually, adding curtly, 'Holiday.'

'What for?' Manju asked. 'And didn't that boy next
door, what's his name, go to school? Have they declared a
special holiday for you?'

'Sssh,' Vasant hissed angrily. 'Will you shut up? I'll go
tomorrow, don't worry,' he added loftily, speaking as if he
would be doing the school a favour by going.

Babu had hoped to question Arvind about yesterday's
incident, but with Vasant sitting there all agog, he decided
he wouldn't open the topic. He needn't have worried.
Vasant immediately jumped right into it. 'Have you heard
what happened? Did you see it? Were you there?' Vasant
began, hoping to lead on to the fact that he himself had
been there and seen all of it. To his disappointment,
however, Arvind seemed disinterested.

'I wasn't there,' Arvind said, yawning. 'But I've heard
the whole story. I'm tired of hearing about it. People don't

seem to have anything else to talk about today. It was all very stupid, if you ask me.'

'It wasn't,' Manju said indignantly. She hadn't realized, as Babu had instantly done, that Arvind was pretending. 'It was exciting and very brave. I wonder who those men were!'

'I wonder,' Arvind repeated after her, but in an entirely disinterested tone. And now, something in Arvind's blank face, his dull tone, told Manju too, that Arvind didn't really wonder. He knew.

'Arvind, was it . . .' she began, but a look from him warned her.

Babu adroitly barged in, so that there was no awkward moment of silence. 'Arvind,' he said, 'Annu-kaka says the police will trouble people here now. Do you think so?'

'Of course!' Arvind said emphatically. 'Won't take much time for the pack of hunters to jump on us now.'

'Let them come,' Vasant said bravely. 'We'll . . . we'll . . .'

'We'll do our lessons,' Arvind completed the sentence. 'Manju and Vasant, you start with Arithmetic.'

'Me!' Vasant asked in astonishment.

'Yes, that's what you're here for, aren't you?' Arvind said coolly.

Vasant had thought it would be fun to have lessons with Arvind instead of in school. He changed his mind now. Arvind was strict and businesslike. Vasant twitched, sighed, and changed positions endlessly. 'Worse than school,' he grumbled to Babu and Manju on the way back. 'Only three of us and he never takes his eyes off you even for a second. At least in school, there are many of us.'

By evening, rumours were rife that a big police saheb would be coming to Narayanpur with a large police force. The next morning a D.S.P. did, in fact, arrive to question people about the incident. For some reason, Vasant seemed to believe he would be one of those questioned by the police. He waited impatiently for the summons, meanwhile rehearsing what he would say to them.

'Fool!' Babu said angrily. 'Idiot! Go and tell the police everything. Tell them the names of the persons who did it. Go and help the police to arrest them as well. You want to be a traitor, don't you?'

Vasant's jaw sagged. 'I never thought of it that way!' he said lamely. He had only thought of the importance it would give him, being summoned by the police.

Manju sighed loudly and dramatically. 'That's the trouble with you—you never think. You've got sawdust where your brains should be. Maybe cowdung too. Sometimes I get a funny smell from your head.' And she sniffed.

'You . . . you . . . .' Vasant fumed. 'If you weren't a girl, I'd . . . .'

'You'd what?' Manju taunted him. 'Come on: even if I'm a girl I'm not scared. Come and hit me—come on.'

As Manju jumped about and Vasant glared at her, they heard the front door close with a bang. The children immediately stopped their sparring and looked at one another in surprise. The front door was never closed until bedtime. Who could it be?

It was Annu-kaka who came in, still wearing his slippers. He entered, looked down at his feet, and flung the slippers angrily out of the door. The children looked at Annu-kaka's face, at his slippers flying out and again at each other. A mystery!

'Annu-kaka!' Amma had rushed out on hearing the door bang. 'What is it?'

'Appa?' Vanamala-auntie asked apprehensively as Annu-kaka now flung his turban away. It fell into Vasant's hands and Vasant mechanically and neatly caught it and then stared at it in surprise as if wondering how it came to be there. Manju began to giggle at the look on his face.

'What is it? I'll tell you what it is,' Annu-kaka said angrily. 'I'm now expected to be a Mir Jafar, a traitor to my own country . . . .'

The women and children stared at Annu-kaka as if he

had gone crazy. Annu-kaka and Mir Jafar? What was the connection? Then Babu understood. Mir Jafar was the traitor who had helped the British against his own countrymen.

'Just because I've kept to myself and my work, he thinks I'm going to become a spy for him, does he?'

'Who, Appa?' Vanamala-auntie asked, taking the turban from Vasant's hands. Vasant had now begun stroking it as if it was a cat or something. Manju thought he looked ridiculous.

'That rotter of a policeman. The Deputy Superintendent or whatever he is. Can you imagine what he suggested I do? Oh, he was polite all right. Talking smooth and easy as if we were the best of friends. "I know you're a man of sense and understanding," he said. "I know you don't approve of all these senseless acts of violence. I'm sure you agree with me that Gandhism is just another name for lawlessness and violence. We've heard some of the rogues are hiding somewhere in this area. We'll be most grateful if you let us know if you hear about their whereabouts. Or if you know anyone who's helping them. We won't ever forget your help, you can be sure of that!" Tchah!' Annu-kaka made a sound, showing complete disgust and contempt.

No, they'd never seen Annu-kaka in such a foul temper before. It took him a long time to calm down, and even then they could see him simmering. After lunch he seemed in a better mood. He was relaxing on the thin mattress in the front hall, leaning against the large fat bolster, a paan box before him, when someone came in shouting, 'Annappa, Annappa.' Annu-kaka paused in the act of pushing a paan into his mouth.

'Annappa,' an excited face looked in and an excited voice spoke, 'they've arrested Mahadevappa.'

'What!' Annu-kaka pushed the paan in and his moustache began to move up and down as he chewed it rapidly.

'They've taken him to the police station. The Sub-Inspector has taken him.'

'Mmmph, mmmph,' Annu-kaka mumbled through a mouthful of paan as he sprang to his feet.

'They say he was the leader of the thing that happened yesterday.'

'Idiots!' Annu-kaka said. He snatched his turban off the peg, and pushing it down on his head, walked out.

'Vasya!' Vanamala-auntie yelled, seeing Vasant dashing after him. 'Where are you going?'

'To see what's happening,' Vasant called out over his shoulder.

Vanamala-auntie followed the boys to the door and yelled, 'Vasya, Babu, come home.'

Annu-kaka heard the shouts and looking back briefly said, 'Boys, go home. Stay there, both of you.'

Vasant scowled at his mother as they reluctantly turned back. 'Why did you have to yell? Look how you've gone and spoiled everything.' Vanamala-auntie, seeing that he would now stay at home, ignored him and went in.

'I say, Vasant,' Babu said a little later. 'Tell you what, let's just go on the road and see if anything's happening.'

Manju, who with Shanti was playing with tamarind seeds, looked up frowning. 'Vanamala-auntie said you mustn't go.'

The two boys made furious faces at her. 'Now, don't open your mouth and blab. Who asked you to poke your nose in? You want to be a . . . ' Vasant brought it out grandly, with almost as much force as Annu-kaka had done, ' . . . a Mir Jafar?'

Manju put out her tongue at them. 'Go and get into trouble. Who cares!'

Babu was quite confident she wouldn't tell on them. The women were having their food in the kitchen as they sneaked out. The road was deserted.

As they walked towards the police station, Vasant told Babu about Mahadevappa. He was an old man, a

Gandhian, who had taken part in the Salt Satyagraha. He had been badly injured by a police lathi at that time and for a while had been almost crippled. He had then come back to Narayanpur and taken up other activities like spinning khadi, working among the poor villagers and helping the Harijans—all Gandhiji's favourite programmes. He was much loved by the people, not only of Narayanpur, but of all the villages around, and was always ready to give his help to anyone who needed it.

'Imagine arresting him!' Vasant said. 'He wouldn't even hurt a fly. As if he would organize yesterday's raid!'

When they reached the police station, they found Annu-kaka, the Vakil and some other prominent men of Narayanpur standing on the open verandah of the police station, arguing with an officer. A few constables, armed with rifles, watched stolidly. The news of Mahadevappa's arrest had spread and there were already a number of people around the police station. Even as the boys stood there—a safe distance from Annu-kaka's eyes—the small number became a crowd. The narrow lane was soon full of people watching the drama silently. There was no pushing or talking, just people staring intently at the arguing men. Finally the Vakil threw his hands up in a gesture of resignation, fixed his cap firmly on his head, and turned round as if to leave. He seemed startled to see so many people standing there and staring.

'What happened, Vakil saheb?' someone shouted.

The Vakil made a negative gesture with his right hand and suddenly the atmosphere changed. The crowd—it was still growing—lost its quality of quiet listening and became, in a moment, turbulent and threatening.

'Mahadevappa,' a voice cried out, 'let him go.'

'Let him go, let him go,' a number of voices took up the chant. In a minute the crowd surged forward, taking up the cry: 'Mahadevappa, let him go, let him go.'

All at once the Sub-Inspector, and the other men found

themselves in the midst of a mob. The policemen who had till then stood like statues, now began to act—pushing the people back, shoving with their hands, their backs, their rifles. It was no use. They might as well have tried to stop a river in flood.

'Babu, here, here,' Vasant was screaming in a shrill voice. He had nimbly climbed up the wall of the police station and was standing triumphantly on the domed pillars from where he had a splendid view. Unfortunately others, including Annu-kaka, had an equally splendid view of him. 'Vasant!' Annu-kaka's roar startled him so much he almost lost his balance. 'Get down from there, get down at once.'

As Vasant rapidly slithered down, Babu noticed that the crowd had now pushed the policemen back into the building. The door closed behind them. The men began to bang on the door calling out, 'Mahadevappa, let him go, let him go.'

Vasant tried to wriggle his way through to Babu. The crowd was now both boisterous and aggressive. Abuses were flung at the police. Annu-kaka and the Vakil struggled to say something to the people, holding up their hands as if pleading for quiet, but nothing could be heard except the monotonous chant of the crowd.

The boys who had retreated, were now wedged against the small front door of a house in the lane. Vasant, to Babu's astonishment, suddenly turned round and flung himself at the door, screaming, 'Kittya, Kittya, open the door, it's me, Vasant.'

In response to his frantic hammering, the door was cautiously opened and an eye gleamed suspiciously at them through a narrow slit. 'Who is it?' a quavery voice asked. Vasant impatiently threw himself on the door and fell through it into the house, Babu following on his heels, before the person behind the door could recover himself. Vasant shouting excitedly, 'Here, Babu, this way,' raced up a narrow, open, white-washed flight of stairs. A little door led to the roof of the house. Grass grew in wild profusion and there were two chimneys. Babu and Vasant stood against a chimney and stared at the scene below.

There was Annu-kaka forcibly dragging away some of the men, shouting, gesticulating. There were others too who, like him, were trying to calm down the people, to stop them from banging, on the door, but it was sheer chaos. As Annu-kaka and the others pushed some men off the verandah, others jumped up and took their place.

A boy now joined them saying, 'Vasya! I thought it was you. My grandfather is having a fit downstairs. He was trying to prevent us from going out, and you rushed in like that.'

'Look,' Babu clutched at Vasant's arm, 'the Sub-Inspector has come out.'

There was an immediate hush. In a short while, the Sub-Inspector went back in, followed by some of the men. The shouting and hammering stopped. Instead, groups of men stood around talking. Within ten minutes the men came out. With them was a little old man in a white shirt, dhoti and Gandhi cap. At once there was a loud cry of: 'Mahadevappa, Mahadevappa!' The cry was taken up by everyone.

It was a triumphant chorus and the Sub-Inspector stood there silently, watching the people carry their hero away. He looked a defeated and dejected man.

The boys raced down the stairs, Kittya with them, past the old man who watched them with an astonished face, and joined the crowd on the road. They went along with the shouting, cheering crowd for a while, then ran home hoping to get there before Annu-kaka did.

They reached home flushed and excited, and before anyone could say anything about their having disobeyed orders, they blurted out the happenings at the police station.

Annu-kaka came in a little later, looking exhausted, but somehow pleased with himself. This time he put his slippers and turban away neatly before going in to wash. He came back wiping his hands and face, and picking up his huge glass of water, drank all of it in one gulp. Then, with a loud sigh, he relaxed against the bolster.

'You heard what happened, eh?' he asked Amma.

'All of it,' Amma smiled. 'These two boys . . . . '

His eyes fell on Babu and Vasant. 'Yes, these fellows. Didn't I tell you both to stay at home?' But there was no anger in his voice—he seemed to be in an unusually good mood. 'I never imagined the people would be in such a violent mood.'

'But Annu-kaka, why did they arrest Mahadevappa?' Manju asked.

'Because they're idiots!' Annu-kaka said. 'Imagine saying he's the leader of the underground movement and that he organized the raid on the Treasury! "If he's the leader, so am I," I said to the Sub-Inspector. And the fool thought I really meant it. He would have arrested me as well, if the Vakil hadn't dinned some sense into his thick skull.'

Annu-kaka was in an unusually talkative mood that evening. Some friends came in and the talk went on. When they had all gone, Ajji came out to ask, 'Will you have your dinner now?'

'Dinner is ready, eh? Good, good. I thought everyone was so busy fighting the British, no one had time to cook!'

They had scarcely begun when, for the second time that day, they heard a commotion. Running footsteps again. Many feet, but no voices, no cries. Just an eerie silence apart from the sound of running feet. Annu-kaka stopped eating, sat up and said, 'What's that!'

'What is it?' Amma asked.

'People running. Timma!'

'I'll find out, don't get up,' Amma said, walking out briskly. They heard her conversing with Timma who was in the cattleshed. When she came back, her face showed consternation.

'There's a fire,' she said, staring at Annu-kaka.

'Fire? Where?'

'The police station—it's burning. Someone has set it on fire.' The children stared at Annu-kaka who, with his hand half-way between his plate and his mouth, stared blankly ahead of him. Vasant, his eyes gleaming with excitement, tried to get up, when Annu-kaka, still staring ahead, snapped, 'Sit down!'

Vasant slumped back into his seat, looking dumbly at Annu-kaka. The thought in all their minds was—what would Annu-kaka do now?

Unbelievable though it seemed, it appeared as if he would do nothing at all. In a few seconds he resumed eating. He didn't say a word until he had finished.

And even then, the only thing he said was, 'No one is to go out of the house. Not on any account.' And with a glare at Vasant, he went out of the room.

The next morning the boys hung about until Annu-kaka left. Vasant, keeping a sharp look-out, immediately whispered in Babu's ear, 'He's gone.' Instantly they made for the police station.

It was a gruesome sight. The building had been almost totally gutted. Only a few smoke-blackened walls still stood, looking both pathetic and terrible. An unpleasant smell hung over the place. Curiously, people didn't seem inclined to stand and stare at the sight. Those going past gave one look, then hurried away with averted faces. It gave Babu a queer feeling to look at it too.

A strange silence lay over Narayanpur that day, in contrast to the noisy scenes that had taken place the previous day. All kinds of rumours flew about in hushed whispers. The Government would take revenge on them, the police would come, the military too—people seemed to enjoy piling on the horrors. A pall of fear lay over them.

Arvind came to them in the evening. 'Is your mother at home?' he asked Babu. He seemed to be in a hurry. Amma went out to where Arvind stood near the tulsi platform. Babu, sitting in the open hall, could not hear them, but he could see them. As Arvind began, Amma's hands went to her mouth—astonishment or horror?—and her eyes grew large. Then, as he went on her face wore a look of concentration that told Babu that she was thinking furiously.

'No,' Babu heard her say once, 'not fair to Annu-kaka.'

A little later she said something which seemed to relieve Arvind because, for the first time, he smiled. Then he went away. As soon as Amma came in, Babu asked her, 'Amma, what is it?'

'Arvind, had a problem,' she said.

'Is it about Mohan?'

Mohan had been very much on Babu's mind since he had known that Sadanand was operating in their area. He was all the while hoping that Mohan would get in touch with them somehow, perhaps even meet them.

'Mohan!' Amma's face was both surprised and wistful. 'No, nothing to do with Mohan. What gave you that idea? Don't worry, Babu, I'll tell you about it later.'

'Tomorrow?' Babu asked hopefully.

'Maybe,' she smiled. 'Let's see what tomorrow brings.'

Tomorrow? They woke up to the sounds of stamping feet and shouted orders, whistles and loud knocks on the door. It was the police. They had cordoned off Narayanpur and were to conduct a house-to-house search.

'No one is to leave the house on any account,' a policeman told them and went out.

'Oh my God!' Amma exclaimed, looking terrified.

'What is it, Sonu? What is it?' Annu-kaka asked anxiously.

'It's Sadanand,' she said in a whisper, her face pale, her eyes large and anxious. 'He's in Timma's house. I told Arvind to take him there. Oh, poor Timma! Oh God, what have I done?'

X

AMMA SEEMED ON the brink of tears. The children stared at her aghast, and even Annu-kaka looked dumbfounded. Then, recovering himself, he said in a low voice, 'Let's not talk here. Come in.'

'I'll never forgive myself if anything happens to Timma,' Amma said, her chin trembling.

'Now, now,' Annu-kaka said in a brisk and businesslike tone. 'Tell me all of it. And fast.'

'Arvind came here last evening,' Amma began in a dull voice. 'He said it was Sadanand—you know him? And you know that Mohan works with him?' she asked Annu-kaka who nodded rapidly twice. 'He said it was Sadanand who led the raid on the Treasury that day. He got hurt in the action—a rifle or lathi gave him a bad blow on his leg. He's been hiding here and there ever since. Yesterday they heard there's likely to be a search in some houses. Sadanand was in one of the houses mentioned. And so Arvind wanted to move Sadanand somewhere else. Sangya's been helping them too.' Annu-kaka's face didn't change, not a bit, as Amma went on: 'Arvind said Sangya suggested taking Sadanand to Sannur. I thought it wouldn't be fair to have him there without your knowledge. Then I thought of Timma. After all, he's Sangya's nephew. I never thought, I never imagined they would search all the houses.' Her voice faltered and died away.

'Hummph!' Annu-kaka looked grave and solemn and began walking briskly up and down the room, his hands behind his back, obviously thinking furiously. The children looked at him hopefully. Surely he would find a way out of this!

Abruptly he walked out of the room. 'I'll try to meet the Sub-Inspector,' he mumbled as he went. But he was back almost immediately. 'No use. They won't let us get out.'

Amma sat down as if her legs had suddenly given way. A loud knock at the door startled all of them. Vasant ran to open it and came back with a scared look on his face, followed by two policemen and one officer.

'We have to search the house,' the officer said.

'Go ahead,' Annu-kaka said briefly. 'I know I can't stop you.'

Amma got up and walked in quickly to prepare Ajji for the search. The policemen's entry had given her back her resolution and courage. She looked determined once more.

The men made a thorough search, even going into the puja room, at which the normally mild Ajji rushed out in a fury. 'They're . . . look . . . stop!' she stammered. Annu-kaka in a few words restrained her from saying any more. She stood there, her chest heaving, her eyes glittering with anger. Vanamala-auntie put her arm around her and took her away.

After what seemed to them a very long time, it was over and the men left. 'Annu-kaka,' Amma said, looking as if she had made up her mind, 'I've been thinking . . .'

And now there was another knock at the door. No, not one knock, but a kind of frantic hammering. Annu-kaka walked out and reached the door in a few long strides. He had scarcely unbolted the door when Timma fell in, almost at his feet. 'Sahukar, Sahukar, save me, help me.'

Amma, her mouth open in horror, ran to him. What had they done, what were they going to do to Timma? She wouldn't let them, she would take all the blame on herself, after all, she was responsible . . . .

But Timma, now raised up by Annu-kaka, was wailing loudly, beating his breast and sobbing out, 'He's dead, my grandfather is dead!'

Annu-kaka said in an unbelieving voice, 'Your grandfather? Dead?'

Babu saw Timma flash a sudden look at Annu-kaka before sobbing once again, 'Yes, he's gone, the old man . . . he's gone.'

And now they noticed an armed policeman standing behind Timma, watching the scene with the greatest interest.

'And they won't let us have the funeral,' Timma went on, his body and voice shaking with his sobs. 'He died early in the morning, Sahukar, and they won't let us take him away. They wouldn't even let me come here to you. I want . . . I want . . .' Timma, seemingly overcome by grief, couldn't go on.

Annu-kaka patted him on the back and said, 'Poor old man, I never knew he was so bad.'

Timma's grief-stricken face came out of the end of his turban and he said, 'Why, even last night he was talking and he spoke of you, Sahukar.'

The policeman nodded sympathetically and leaned against the wall, his arms folded across his chest.

'And I knew you would give us money for the funeral. How can we poor people have so much money in the house? But they wouldn't let me come to you, and he's lying there . . . .' Timma began wailing again.

'Oh, is that all? Come on, Timma, take heart. The poor old man—he had to go some time.' Annu-kaka wiped his eyes with his sleeve. 'Come inside, I'll give you the money. Where are you?' he called out to Ajji who was looking on with a bewildered face. 'Get the keys of the safe. Where's Vana? She has them.'

And ignoring the policeman, Annu-kaka gently led Timma into the house. The moment they were in, Timma moved respectfully away from Annu-kaka, and stood, quiet and serious as always. There was no trace of grief on his face now. Vanamala-auntie came in jingling the keys. 'Open the safe, Vana,' Annu-kaka whispered. 'See that you make a lot of noise doing it. Now then,' he beckoned to

Timma to come closer. Timma squatted on the ground near Annu-kaka. 'Where is he?'

'At home. He asked me to come and tell Avva,' he looked at Amma, 'this story of my grandfather being dead.'

'Timma,' Amma barely breathed the words, 'is he all right?'

'Yes,' Timma smiled briefly. 'He's dressed as a woman, in a sari and bangles and all that. He's crying too, for my grandfather.'

'And your grandfather?' Annu-kaka asked in a puzzled voice, while Amma, who seemed to have understood, gave a broad smile.

Timma grinned too. 'He's lying still on the ground, pretending to be dead.'

Annu-kaka's face lit up with understanding. 'Oh, I see. A mock funeral.'

'That's right,' Amma smiled back.

'Well,' Annu-kaka sat back. 'We'll get him out of here. I'll go to the Deputy Superintendent and see that he gives me permission to take out a funeral procession. Where's Sangya?'

'He's at home, howling and wailing and seeing that no one goes too close to the "dead body".'

'All right, Timma, you come with me to the Deputy Saheb.'

'And I,' Amma said, getting up briskly, 'will go and comfort poor Gangavva.' Gangavva was Timma's mother and Sangya's sister.

'If the police let you go to her,' Annu-kaka reminded her.

'They had better,' Amma retorted. Manju and Babu were glad to see that her fighting spirit was back.

They all went out, Timma looking sorrowful once more. The policeman was still standing there, his rifle now leaning against the wall, a bored look on his face.

'Come on, you,' Annu-kaka said to him contemptuously,

'we're going to your Saheb. You and your rifle can follow us if you want.'

Amma was the first to return, nearly four hours later. Manju, Babu and Vasant, who had been waiting impatiently, flung themselves at her. 'What happened?'

'They've taken him away.' A smile twitched her lips. 'As soon as they left, I came away.'

'Now, Sonu,' Ajji said, 'go and have your bath.'

'Bath?'

'Yes, bath. You haven't had your lunch, you know.'

'All right, Kaki. But listen, kids, get yourselves ready. We have to go, too, as soon as Annu-kaka returns.'

'Go? Where?'

'Sannur.'

While she had her lunch, the children plied her with questions about the 'mock funeral'. Amma began to laugh. 'I never knew they could act so well—Sangya, Gangavva, Timma, even Annu-kaka. I believe he went and told the Deputy Saheb: "You're fighting against Hitler, and you use his methods here. One harmless old man is dead, and you won't let his family perform his last rites. I'll see that this news gets about. I'll write to newspapers all over the world. I'll write to His Majesty himself. And the American President."'

'And Sadanand, Amma?'

'Absolutely a weepy female. The old man suddenly felt twitchy once. "The body" began to scratch itself. Thank goodness, there were no outsiders then. The Sannur police-patil came in twice, God knows why. Some policeman peeped in every now and then. Otherwise, no one was allowed. The police counted the number of people who went for the funeral. They're going to count them when they return.'

'But then, how . . .?' Babu asked frowning.

'Just you wait and see.' Amma refused to say any more until Annu-kaka returned.

He came in, looked at all the staring faces, then chuckled. 'Well, we buried the fellow.'

'Really?' Vasant gasped.

'What do you think?' Annu-kaka gave another chuckle. 'Two policemen came along with us. We gave them some money and asked them to have a cup of tea while we did the unpleasant task of burying "the body". A grave had been dug, and we put the old chap in. And then, in a flash—you should have seen how brisk and spry the old man was—the body had joined mourners by his own graveside.'

And Annu-kaka began to laugh. The laughter came from somewhere deep inside him, a rumbling laugh that came in heaves and spurts. It was so infectious a sound that the children began to laugh too, and soon the women joined in. Ajji however, was scandalized, thinking in a confused way, that there had been a funeral and that one shouldn't laugh at such a time.

'So, we're going?' Amma asked Annu-kaka cryptically when they were calmer.

'Yes, after four. The search will be over by then.'

'But where are we going?' Babu asked impatiently.

'I told you. Sannur. I'm going to the Lakshmi Narayan temple there. Today's Friday, isn't it? My day for going to that temple. Go on, get ready quickly.'

As the children scrambled to their feet, she added, 'No, not you, Vasant.'

Vasant stopped and stared at Amma aghast. Not him! It wasn't true! She didn't mean it! When he realized that she and Annu-kaka *did* mean it, he was indignant, and hurt, so terribly hurt that Manju pleaded, 'Please, Amma, let him come.'

'Well,' Amma said doubtfully, looking at Vasant's face, which looked hopefully back at her. 'You'll talk and tell everyone about it,' she said finally.

'Me?' Vasant asked in terrific surprise. 'Me talk?'

'Here, Vasya,' Babu pounced on him, 'take an oath.'

'What for?' Vasant turned bewildered eyes on him.

'Promise, swear, take a solemn oath that you won't say a word to anyone.'

'About what?'

'Anything, everything. Take it, you ass. If you want to come along, give us your promise and *keep it,*' Babu said in an awful voice. 'Or else, I'll . . . .'

'I promise, I swear . . . .' Vasant began gabbling, his hair almost standing up in his excitement.

'That's enough,' Amma said laughing.

'Come on, then,' Vasant rammed his cap on his head and ran out.

'Wait,' Annu-kaka caught hold of him. 'Timma has to come.'

'And no monkey tricks, mind,' Vanamala-auntie said.

'Do I ever play any monkey tricks?' Vasant asked in a hurt voice. 'And why only me?'

But he was grinning when Timma and the cart arrived. Once inside however, looking at Amma's grave face, he subsided into the utmost seriousness. He became even more solemn when Amma told them that they were to pick up a 'passenger' and take him to Sannur.

'Has Sangya passed the message, Timma?' Amma asked.

'Yes, Avva, long ago.'

After quite a while, when they were closer to Sannur than to Narayanpur, Amma said, 'Timma, stop here.'

They waited in silence. It was so quiet—only a bird going whoo-whoo somewhere—that Manju imagined she could hear their hearts beating. Then there was a rustle in the bushes by the roadside and a man came limping out. Timma jumped down, helped the man into the cart and got up himself. Clicking his tongue and laying his whip lightly over the backs of the bulls, he started the cart again. They hadn't paused for more than two minutes.

Now the cart seemed crowded. There was a strong smell,

too, the smell of unwashed clothes. The children stared curiously at their 'passenger'. There was no need for Amma to hide it any longer. They knew it was Sadanand. He was dressed like any villager in a grimy dhoti, a ragged shirt and turban on his head. He was, however, clean-shaven, because, they guessed, he had been a 'woman' that morning. He was sweating and panting when he got in, but soon recovered himself and smiled at them. He greeted Amma, then looked at the three of them.

'This is Babu,' Amma said.

'And Manju,' he said, smiling at Manju. 'And this is . . .?' He cocked his head and looked enquiringly at Vasant.

'Vasant,' the other two chorused.

'Vasant. Annarao's grandson, eh?'

Vasant, still staring dumbly, said nothing. Again it was Babu and Manju who replied, 'Yes.'

'Dumb boy, eh? Or too shy?'

Manju giggled at that, while Vasant went on staring. 'He's scared, that's what he is,' Babu grinned. 'We made him swear he wouldn't open his mouth and so he's . . .'

' . . . not opening his mouth,' Sadanand completed the sentence. 'Good boy. But it's all right now, you can open your mouth. Here, let me unlock it for you.' And Sadanand mimicked the turning of a key in a lock in front of Vasant's face. 'There!'

Vasant let out a huge sigh and began to laugh.

'Timma,' Amma said in a low voice, 'take us to the house first, then we'll go to the temple.'

Timma drew the cart very close to the house, and after the others had alighted, he helped Sadanand to get down. Sadanand hobbled in very quickly and then sat down, his face showing that he was in pain.

'Is it hurting a lot?' Amma asked anxiously.

'A bit,' he said, making a wry face. 'I'll be all right now. You go ahead.'

Amma seemed reluctant, but she had to go. She was supposed to have come here to visit the temple; it would look odd if she didn't go there at all. 'All right. But you . . . .'

'I'll stay here with him, Amma,' Babu said.

'No,' Sadanand said. 'Not really necessary.'

'I think it's a good idea. Babu, you stay here. We'll be back soon. Manju, Vasya, come on.'

'Look, Babu,' Sadanand said when they had gone, 'you mustn't stay in here with me. Go out, and if anyone comes you don't know who I am, or that I was here at all. Okay?'

Babu gave him some water to drink and made him comfortable before going out. He looked in once or twice, but Sadanand seemed to be sleeping. Babu roamed about restlessly, not straying too far from the house. In a short while, the evening hush fell over the place. The voices of two men who were carrying on a conversation some distance away came to Babu clearly and distinctly.

After what seemed ages he heard the creaking of the returning cart. Vasant jumped off even before it stopped and raced towards Babu. The dust spurted from his running feet. 'Is he all right?' he panted when he reached Babu.

'Yes. Why?'

'There was a policeman near the temple. He looked suspiciously at us. I stared back at him. If he had tried anything, I would have . . . I was just waiting for him to start something. I'd have shown him.'

The cart stopped. Manju jumped out, holding her skirts high. 'Did Vasant tell you about the policeman? Is he all right?'

'Yes.'

'My God, I was so scared when I saw that policeman . . . .'

'I wasn't.'

'You were.'

'I wasn't.'

'Liar!'

'Did anyone come here?' Amma interrupted them.

'No one.'

'Thank goodness.'

Timma untethered the bullocks and they sank to the ground, their jaws crunching the straw, bits of foam showing at the corners of their mouth.

In a short while it was dark. They could just see a tiny glow that was the end of Timma's beedi. A little later they saw a small point of light in the distance. It became larger and as it drew closer, there was Sangya on a bike, and another man with him.

'They've come,' Amma said, only now showing the strain she had been under. 'Sangya?' she called out softly.

'Amma,' the other man said, getting off his bike and leaning it against the wall.

'Mohan!' Amma exclaimed. And even as Babu and Manju stared, he walked quickly into the house. They ran in after him. Sangya was lighting the lantern. Once the lantern was lit, they could see Mohan. If they'd seen him first instead of hearing his voice, they'd never have recognized him. He was dressed like a villager, his face was dark, and he had grown a bushy moustache.

Manju asked in an unbelieving voice, 'Mohan, is it you?'

'Yes,' he said, tweaking her plait playfully. 'Really me, Manju.'

And then he went over to Sadanand and said a few words to him. When he came back, he sat cross-legged opposite Amma. The lantern was behind him and his shadow loomed on the opposite wall. 'Amma,' he smiled and his teeth looked extraordinarily white in his dark face. 'And Babu—you've really grown, man. And Vasya, too. How's life, Vasya?'

'Wonderful,' Vasant grinned back. 'No school. I say, Mohan,' Vasant seemed to be bursting with excitement, 'can I come with you?'

'Where?'

'Wherever you're going. I'll do anything you say. Please!'

'Not right now. A little later, maybe. You can come in at the end and give the knockout blow to the British. Okay?'

'But, Mohan . . . .'

'And,' Mohan went on, disregarding the interruption, 'if you want to help us right now, go out and stand guard. Let us know if someone is coming.'

Vasant sprang to his feet almost knocking down the lantern in his eagerness. The lantern rocked and Babu just managed to steady it while the shadows swayed and moved fantastically.

'Right! Now . . . .'

In such a short time Mohan had become so confident, so certain of himself that he seemed far older than his eighteen years. Babu and Manju stared at him admiringly. Look how he'd got rid of Vasya! Mohan, as if reading their thoughts, grinned at them. 'I didn't send him out only to get rid of him. I'd have done it in any case. There's an informer somewhere. We haven't been able to find out who it is as yet.'

'Is it safe for you to be here?' Amma asked.

'As safe as anywhere else. Actually, Amma, we've been staying here for long—did you know I was so close by? The police officer here—a chap called Naik—he's one of us. I mean, he's a sympathizer. He came to meet us once. God, that was a bad moment, we were so many, if we'd been caught it would have been a bad blow. We thought we were finished. But no, he came to tell us he would close his eyes to our presence here if we promised not to start any disturbance in his area. We kept our promise. But he was transferred. Only then did we organize the raid on the Treasury.'

'And now, Mohan?'

'Now? It isn't safe here any longer. We have to leave. It's not just us; if we're found here, the local people will be made to suffer. That Superintendent Williams—I tell you, Amma, he's not a man, he's a beast. The kind of things he's doing! Oh, I know there are decent Englishmen and decent policemen. Our Principal, the one before this rotter came, he was a fantastic fellow. And this Naik chap, he even brought us two jars of pickles—a gift from his wife!' Mohan grinned, then became serious again. 'But one man like Williams is bad enough. Do you know he arrested a woman who'd just had a baby because he wanted her husband and the man wasn't there? How long are we going to put up with these things?'

Amma put her hand on Mohan's arm. 'You're right, Mohan. But don't take any unnecessary risks. And no violence.'

'Don't worry, Amma. I've been more non-violent than the Mahatma so far.'

'When will we see you again, Mohan?' Manju asked.

'Some time. Soon, I hope'

'How will you take Sadanand, Mohan?' Babu asked.

'We've got two bikes, Sangya and I. We'll carry him in turns. Tomorrow we'll be away from here. Look after yourselves. And Amma, if you do need to get in touch with me . . .' He bent down and whispered something in Amma's ear. Amma nodded. She sat where she was while the children went out with Mohan and Sadanand.

And then they were gone. Timma looked in and said, 'Shall we go, Avva?'

Amma gave a small sigh and seemed to pull herself out of her faraway thoughts.

'Right, Timma. Here, Babu, take the lantern.' They got back into the cart quiet and subdued, though Manju kept cursing her long skirts which seemed to get entangled everywhere. The cart began lurching back towards Narayanpur. Babu shivered once. 'Cold?' Amma asked. Babu shook his head. It was a bit chilly now, but it wasn't that. Manju knew what it was. He was thinking of the two men cycling away in the dark and of the third man they carried with them. Would they reach their destination—wherever it was—safely? Manju thought of Mohan's words, 'How long are we going to put up with these things?'

Yes, Babu was thinking it too: How long? In their own country they had to sneak like thieves in the night. And what for? Because they wanted to get rid of people who'd no right to be there. It wasn't fair!

'Thank God, there's no moon,' Amma said suddenly, and Babu and Manju knew she was thinking of the three men too.

XI

THE SEARCH WAS over. It had been a failure. Neither in Narayanpur, nor in the other towns and villages, had the police found anything but some old pamphlets and circulars. The police had been thorough; they had searched homes, climbed on roofs, gone down wells. One policeman, who had been lowered into a well to search inside it, had panicked in its damp darkness and had begun splashing about wildly, yelling, 'Get me out, get me out.' How the people had laughed at the story! There was a story of a daring escape too—of a wanted man who had been hiding in a school building when the police had been seen making their way to it. He had escaped through a window, been chased by the police, and got away in the nick of time by climbing from a haystack to the top of a temple. He had lain there, absolutely still, for nearly six hours, in the hot sun. Finally, when it was dark, he had come down and escaped.

The police had been bitterly disappointed at having found nothing worthwhile. Fearful of facing their saheb with nothing to show for their efforts, they had made some arrests, but none of the really active underground workers had been found. Sadanand, Mohan and the others had got away safely. Sangya had brought them the news the next morning and they all heaved a sigh of relief. But there was no time to rejoice. Scarcely a day or two after the search, as if in reply to the police, a dak bungalow where government officers usually stayed, was burnt. To make matters worse, the Superintendent of Police had himself been staying there at the time. The fire had been noticed early and everyone who was inside had been able to get out. But nothing else could be saved. Whispers went round of how the D.S.P., clad in his pyjamas and slippers—his uniform was destroyed in the fire—had run around, fiercely collaring all the poor shivering servants of the Dak Bungalow, frightening them to death, threatening to arrest them, until he came to his senses and realized that, since they hadn't run away, they could not have had anything to do with the fire. His temper didn't improve when he also realized that the actual culprits must have, in the meantime, got away. He went into a frenzy. He would teach these people a lesson, he was said to have threatened.

Only a few days later, the people of Narayanpur learnt the terrible news. The Government had imposed a collective fine of Rs 7,000 on the people of Narayanpur. They would have to pay for their destructive activities, th￼ / were told.

'7,000?' Annu-kaka was thunderstruck. 'Where will this town of poor people get so much money?'

The question was on everyone's lips, but to the Government it made no difference. Pay the money, the people were told, or else their property would be confiscated.

'It's horribly unfair,' Arvind said to Annu-kaka, his face angry and grim. 'They're bleeding us to death. Do you think,' he asked Annu-kaka quietly, 'we should just lie down quietly and die?'

'No!' Annu-kaka roared, clapping one fist into the palm of his other hand. 'No!'

'Then, listen,' Arvind spoke quietly, his face showing no excitement. It was Annu-kaka who changed in a second, from anger to eager excitement; he seemed almost happy.

'Arvind,' he said finally, clapping Arvind on the back, 'you shame us older fellows.'

Babu, who remembered how critical Annu-kaka had been of Arvind, 'that dressed-up dandy', looked on in amazement. How Annu-kaka had changed!

'Anything is better than just taking things lying down,' he went on. 'Now, let's see how the others feel about it.'

There was no doubt at all about what the others felt. It was as if a torch had been lit somewhere, bringing a glow, an answering sparkle in people's eyes. The children too soon heard of Arvind's plan. In fact, it was the only thing people could talk of. Arvind's idea was simply this—that the people of Narayanpur would resist the Government order. They would not pay the fine. Instead, they would hold a public meeting in which they would declare themselves to be independent. And they would announce that as free citizens of a free country, they would obey no orders of a foreign government.

In reply the Government declared a ban on any public meeting or a gathering of more than four persons. But how little the people of Narayanpur cared about such things now! Babu remembered how he had despaired—would these people never do anything? Now it seemed the time had come for them to do something.

'Babu,' Manju said suddenly one day, 'do you remember Amma saying once—it's as if a sleeping tiger has been awakened?'

Yes, Babu did remember that.

'It's like that now in Narayanpur, isn't it?'

It was. The mood of the people had changed. People read pamphlets and circulars telling them what people in other parts of the country were doing. They read of Government brutality, of the people's courage. They had seen with their own eyes, during the search, how men and women had been abused, beaten and dragged off to jail on flimsy grounds. They had watched the police enter their homes and throw their things about. They would not forget these things. And so they were, almost all of them, behind Arvind and his plan.

Arvind had come out into the open now. He was a most active leader. Even his brother the Vakil, who had, like

Annu-kaka, scorned him, listened respectfully to his words. The children's lessons had all but come to an end; Arvind rarely had the time. Nevertheless, they went to him every day. There was work for them to do as well—carrying messages from home to home and running all kinds of errands.

Miraculously, the women too were involved this time in the agitation. 'You must try and make them join in,' Arvind had told Amma. And Amma had begun visiting the women, talking to them, persuading them, explaining to them. 'When there is so much work to be done, will we sit in front of our fires thinking of nothing but what to cook for the next meal?' she asked them.

Some women found it difficult to accept the idea that they could be of any use outside their homes. But many others, specially the younger women and older girls, responded enthusiastically to Amma's talk. They were thrilled by the thought of being of some use to their country.

Soon the anti-government fever was at its height. Anyone who had anything to do with the government, specially a person who wore a uniform, became a hated figure. People were forced to give up government jobs. Village records were burnt. One rich landlord announced that he was giving up his title of Rao Bahadur which had been given to him by the British. Everyone began to wear a Gandhi cap. In Narayanpur, these white caps blossomed overnight. Even Annu-kaka put away his bulky turban and wore a Gandhi cap. He looked a different man altogether, softer, not so stern, and yet purposeful. But there were many, specially government servants, who were scared to wear these caps but they were often forced to do so. For the children it became a kind of game, and the more the person resisted, the more exciting and fascinating the game became.

Babu, Manju and Vasant first saw the children at it one morning. Hearing shrill yells and the barking of dogs they

ran out of the house, and saw the Sannur police-patil cycling away for dear life, followed by a horde of screaming children. While they watched, some children ran out of a house ahead of him and got hold of his cycle as he came up to them. The cycle rocked and he fell off. In a flash he was surrounded by a crowd of delighted children. The man struggled, managed to get out of their hands and ran into Annu-kaka's house shouting, 'Sahukar, help me, save me.'

Some of the children chased him in and catching hold of him tried to put the white cap on his head, but he kept jumping nimbly from side to side, foiling their attempts. He caught sight of Amma and Vanamala-auntie who had come out to see what the commotion was about. 'Avva, Avva, help me,' he yelled to them frantically. They watched him silently, Amma's face clearly showing her contempt for the man who looked at the Gandhi cap with terrified eyes, as if it was a snake.

Babu, furious now, rushed forward, and snatching the cap from a boy's hand, jammed it down firmly on the police-patil's head. The man, realizing that it was no use struggling, stood still, while the children clapped and laughed. And then, suddenly, he wrenched himself out of their hands and flew out of the house. He grabbed his bike and pedalled away frantically. Some of the children started chasing him all over again, but Babu called out, 'Let him go.'

Sangya, who heard of the incident when he came from Sannur in the evening, seemed worried. 'He's a nasty man, that one,' he told Amma. 'He's always spying on people. Do you know, Avva, he tried to find out where our people were hiding?'

'Our people? You mean Mohan and the others?'

'Hunh!' Sangya removed his turban, got a beedi out of it, looked at it thoughtfully, then vigorously scratched himself behind the ear with it. 'He was always hovering about me, asking questions. That day of the search, he came twice to Timma's place, sniffing like a dog. That's why we sent the old man away to his other daughter's house the very next day. He's a spy, that man, spying for the police.'

'But Sangya,' Vanamala-auntie seemed shocked, 'do you mean to say he would give away our own people?'

'Why not? That fellow will sell his own mother if he can make some profit out of it. Tchah!' And Sangya spat on the ground, showing his utter contempt. 'He hopes the Sarkar will reward him with a big job. That's what he told me too. Hah!'

Vasant suddenly began to laugh. 'He looked comic today, didn't he, Babu? The way he kept hopping, he looked like a circus clown didn't he? What a fool! I'm sure he won't come to Narayanpur for some time now. He'll be ashamed to show his face.'

But Vasant was wrong. The police-patil turned up the very next day, a day which Narayanpur would never forget. It was just a day before the meeting and procession. The Sannur police-patil wasn't alone this time. He swaggered down the street in the midst of five policemen and a Sub-Inspector, full of his own importance though the only persons to see him were some children playing in the street. And they were too engrossed to notice either the police-patil or the men who were with him.

In fact, he would have gone past unnoticed if a little boy hadn't run into him. The child, dressed in a shirt that came down to his knees and nothing else, was rolling a cycle tyre along. As he ran across the road after it, he ran smack into the police-patil. The man almost fell, then recovered himself and cuffed the little boy, who was getting up from the ground where he had fallen. 'Can't you see where you're going? Can't you look, you idiot, or have you no eyes at all, you son of an idiot?'

The little boy, scared by this angry voice, burst into loud sobs. His elder brother, playing marbles nearby, looked up on hearing the howl and ran up to his brother, shouting, 'What's the matter with you? Why are you howling?'

'Your brother, eh?' The police-patil was trying to recover some of the dignity and importance he imagined he had lost when he stumbled. 'Why do you let him play on the roads? Keep him at home.'

Just then, one of the other boys, who had come up to see what the matter was, yelled, 'It's him. I say, here he is. Change his cap, fellows. Change his cap. Give him a Gandhi cap. Don't let him get off this time.'

The next moment, the boys, recognizing the man and eager to continue the exciting game of the other day, ran to him in glee. The man gave a yell of rage. The other policemen who had gone a little ahead, looked back.

'Saheb, saheb,' the police-patil shouted angrily, still trying to fight off the excited, screaming boys. 'Come and help me.'

The Sub-Inspector marched back importantly, the constables a little behind him.

'Hit them, saheb, hit them,' the police-patil screamed.

The Sub-Inspector, ignoring the police-patil, began pushing the children aside, trying to extricate the furious little man from their midst. But more children had come running, eager to join in the exciting game. One of the boys now shouted, 'Remove the policemen's caps. Make them wear Gandhi caps.'

'Take off your caps, policemen, take off your caps,' the children chanted. It was still a game for them. They were laughing and dancing round the policemen in excitement.

But the police-patil was now in an uncontrollable rage. He began hitting out viciously at any one he could lay his hands on. A little girl, who was kicked by him, fell down and lay there among the trampling feet. She gave a feeble scream which her mother, who was sitting on her doorstep, heard.

'My Gangi, my Gangi,' she screamed and ran towards the child who could no longer be seen. In the meantime, one of the boys had managed to get hold of the Sub-Inspector's cap and was waving it about triumphantly.

'Hands off, hands off,' the Sub-Inspector shouted, still trying to keep cool. He waved his stick around. A boy gave a loud cry of pain as it hit him across the jaw. Some boys threw themselves at the Sub-Inspector.

Manju, Shanti, Babu and Vasant, who had gone out on an errand for Arvind, were on their way home when they heard sounds of a commotion.

'Listen,' Babu said. 'Something is going on.'

People had already begun running in the direction of the cries and the children followed.

When they reached the lane, they stood aghast. It was no longer a game. The policemen were viciously hitting out at the children who were screaming, struggling to get away from the cruel blows. Some of the children had fallen down. Suddenly, the watching crowd plunged into the fight, some trying to get the children out, some hitting back at the policemen. The cry of 'They are beating up our children' brought more and more people to the scene.

The adults and the police were now fighting furiously and viciously, the children caught in between. Manju threw herself into the brawl before the others could realize what she was doing. Babu saw her dragging a child away from the trampling feet. Babu darted in too, and so did Vasant, who paused only to shout, 'Shaani!' and he never knew how or why the name he had used for Shanti in his early days, now came back to him. 'Shaani, go get Ajja. Get him fast. Run, run.'

Shanti ran home as fast as she could. As she went she saw Bhima lunging about like an angry bull. And Sangya, too, shouting hoarsely, 'There he is, the spy, Bhimappa, there he is.'

It was utter chaos. There were screams of terror from the children—cries, moans of pain, angry shouts. Babu heard Manju's scream above all these sounds, and almost instantly

Vasant's voice, 'Manju's hurt, Babu.' Babu tried to push himself in, to find out where she was. Blows were raining down on him. He scarcely felt them, so intent was he on getting to Manju. Someone was dragging him away. He tried to resist, to struggle, but he couldn't. 'You're hurt,' he heard a voice say. They propped him against a door and went away. There were sounds of running footsteps. Babu wiped his face. Something was obstructing his vision. His hands came away wet. There was something thick and warm on his face. He stared stupidly at his bloody hands. He could now hear Sangya's voice, and Vasant's, coming as if from a far distance.

'Manju?' he asked, trying to get up.

'It's all right Babu,' Vasant said. 'We've got her.'

Babu slumped back against the door once again. Through the haze that seemed to surround him, he dimly felt that the sounds of commotion were fading away. In fact, it was suddenly peaceful. Babu could hear whispers.

'Are you very hurt, Babu?' That was Annu-kaka's voice. A dull pain had begun now, in addition to the warm blood that was still flowing down his face.

'A little,' he said.

'Can you walk? Shall I help you?'

'I'll take him home, Ajja.'

Vasant put his arm round Babu and helped him home. Amma was waiting. 'Manju?' he asked once again, forgetting that he had already asked about her once.

'She's . . . I think she's broken an arm,' Amma's voice was shaky.

'You go to her, Sonu.' That was Vanamala-auntie. 'We'll look after Babu.'

It was only later that Babu came to know what had happened. It was not just him, with two big gashes on his head; not just Manju, who lay in pain with a broken arm. Nearly a dozen children had been badly injured. One little girl—the one who had fallen down first—had been trampled to death. And, when it was all over, only two policemen had been able to get away. Two lay still and unconscious, one trying feebly to crawl away, moaning and groaning, and two were dead—the Sub-Inspector and the police-patil.

XII

NARAYANPUR WAS SUDDENLY like a ghost town. Even in the daytime, people bolted their doors and stayed inside their homes. There was not a soul on the roads, not a glimmer of light, not a sound, anywhere.

In Annu-kaka's house too, the huge front door had been bolted and barred. Inside, Timma had lit the lamps as usual. He was now milking the cattle and their rustlings could be clearly heard, as also the musical tinkle of the milk streaming into the pail. Manju lay on her bed, quiet and still, her eyes closed, though she was not sleeping. Amma sat by her side, equally silent. Shanti had fallen asleep, her head pillowed on Amma's lap, her body curled up. She was tired and worn out by all the tensions and fears of the day. Ajji and Vanamala-auntie were going on quietly with their cooking, putting the pots and pans down softly, almost without a sound, and speaking only occasionally in whispers.

In contrast to this silence, there was a babble of sound in the front hall. A group of men, almost all the prominent men of Narayanpur, had collected to discuss the day's happenings and to plan their next step. Babu, looking like a wounded soldier, his head swathed in a huge bandage, and Vasant, who had luckily (unluckily, he thought, gazing admiringly at Babu's bandage!) escaped with minor injuries, sat on the steps that led down into the courtyard and listened.

'It's the end,' Annu-kaka said. 'We're in for it now.'

'What will they do?'

'What will they not do?' Arvind countered.

'But, it wasn't our fault, was it? Should we have watched them kill our children?'

'Does it matter whose fault it was?' the Vakil asked dryly. 'We should know by now that we are always in the wrong. The rulers can do no wrong.'

'Bhima,' Annu-kaka said, 'tell us what happened. You were one of the first to be there, weren't you?'

Bhima moved forward on his haunches and said, 'Yes, Sangya and I. It was Gangi's mother who screamed. We heard it and ran and there were the policemen hitting the children. The children were crying out in fright, trying to run away, to protect themselves. But how could they? And there he was—that spy—hitting one little boy. It was he who kicked little Gangi. She cried out and he did not even lift her. He kicked her again, the rotten fellow. I went straight for him . . . .'

'Was it you, Bhima, who hit him?' the Vakil asked, rather sadly, Babu thought.

'Yes,' Bhima said proudly, 'it was me. Sangya wanted to hit him too, but I got him first.'

'Bhima!' Arvind said abruptly. 'You must get away from here. Quickly.'

'Why should I?' Bhima asked scornfully. 'I killed a cockroach—I should be ashamed of that? I should be frightened and run away? When has Bhima run away from anyone?'

Nothing they said could shake him. He was absolutely determined. He would not run away.

'But Sangya must go,' the Vakil said. 'Annappa, send him away.'

Sangya was there, sitting a little distance away from the others, watching them anxiously. At the sound of his name, he got up saying, 'You want me?'

'Yes, Sangya, come here,' Annu-kaka said. Arvind and he took Sangya into the courtyard and they spoke in low tones for a while. Babu and Vasant could see Sangya's head nodding away vigorously. Then Annu-kaka went back to his place and Arvind said, 'Babu, Sangya would like to speak to your mother.'

The boys stood and listened while Sangya told Amma he was going away. 'And if you have any message to give me . . . .' he said. Obviously he was going to join Mohan and the others. 'Arvindappa says not to give me anything in writing. Just tell me what to say.'

Amma blinked, gulped, and seemed to be fighting against tears. Then she composed herself and said, 'Tell him . . . we are all well and happy. Not to worry about us. And to send us news of himself whenever he can. And Sangya . . . don't tell him about all this . . . .' She pointed towards Manju. Sangya nodded. He had a few words with Ajji and Vanamala-auntie before going out. Annu-kaka accompanied him to the door, and just before opening it, put his hand lightly on Sangya's shoulder.

Then Sangya was gone, Timma with him. Annu-kaka stood still for a moment, lifting his cap, scratching his head, looking lost. The next moment he put his cap back on, cleared his throat, and walked back to his place, saying, 'So, is it all decided about tomorrow?'

The men had decided to go on with their earlier plan of a procession and meeting. 'If we back out now, we'll go to jail having achieved nothing. Let's show we aren't afraid. Let's go down fighting,' Arvind had said and most of the others had agreed.

'Yes, it's all clear now,' someone said.

'But,' Arvind said softly, looking round at all the faces, 'if anyone has any doubts or fears, they can stay away. Nobody is forced to join in. We understand.' All eyes met his squarely, all faces showed their determination. Arvind smiled. 'All right,' he said, getting up. 'We've got to be going.'

Quietly, they all dispersed.

'Ajja,' Vasant whispered when they had all gone. 'Can we come too?'

Annu-kaka looked down at the two boys for a moment, then said very seriously, 'No. You boys stay at home. We don't know what's going to happen. I'd like you boys to be here, understand?'

'Yes,' Babu mumbled, getting an inkling of what Annu-kaka was hinting at, but Vasant was not satisfied.

'We're not frightened,' he said.

'Look, Vasya,' Annu-kaka said, unusually gentle, 'it's not that at all. But, don't you think you should be here to help? To do some work? You're old enough to have some sense of responsibility now. Your mothers will need your help . . . .'

Annu-kaka didn't tell them how hard he had had to work to dissuade Amma from joining them. 'I can't back out now,' she had said unhappily, 'not after I've persuaded the women it's their duty to join.'

'You've got to stay back,' Arvind had said. 'There'll be no one else in this house to manage.'

'I may be arrested,' Annu-kaka told the boys bluntly. 'Not "may". I will be arrested.'

'Arrested?' Vasant stared at his grandfather and then said, 'Oh!' He tried to understand that it wasn't just an exciting game any more. Annu-kaka's face was not angry, but sad.

'All right,' Vasant said finally. 'We'll be here.'

The next morning the whole house was up early. It was like Diwali, Babu thought, with all the cheerfulness taken out of it. By the time Annu-kaka had had a bath, Arvind and three others came for him. Annu-kaka put on his cap and looked at his family awkwardly. They were all about him now, even Shanti, rubbing her eyes and yawning. He smiled at her and said, 'Go back to sleep, Shanti.'

'Come back soon, Ajja,' she replied and went off to sleep instantly.

Annu-kaka went to Manju, knelt down by her and said something softly to her. She smiled back at him. 'Vasya,

Babu, be good boys,' he said. He rumpled Vasant's hair, told Babu, 'Take care of yourself,' and with a gruff, 'Well!' for the others, he abruptly walked away. Arvind, with a smile for them, followed.

Then they were gone. They sat in silence and heard the footsteps go past, purposeful and firm. 'Six o'clock,' Vasant said once. 'They will have started by now.'

They heard the story of the procession and what happened later from others. The procession started from Mahadevappa's house, the old man leading it. It was early morning, so early that the mist still clung to the tops of trees and gently cloaked buildings so that their outlines were blurred. Cobwebs sparkled and glittered in the early morning light. Everywhere people stood in doorways, at windows and on roofs, watching the men and a handful of women go past. They walked silent, purposeful and grim, frail old Mahadevappa leading them, the flag held in his hands. They were to hoist the flag when they reached the maidan, after which Mahadevappa would read the resolution. That was the plan.

When they came to the end of the lane which opened out on to the maidan, some figures stepped out from the shadows and stood in front of them. It was a police officer, with his men behind him. There was dead silence. The processionists halted and looked at them.

It was the officer who spoke first. 'I must ask you to disperse,' he said, very polite and formal.

'You have no authority to do so,' Arvind said at once.

Mahadevappa, in a calm voice, said, 'Come men, let's go on.'

'I said, stop,' the officer said, his voice much harsher, much less polite now.

'And I say,' this was Mahadevappa, 'you cannot stop us. We are free citizens of a free country and we insist on our right to proceed. Stand back, all of you.'

'I'm warning you! Take one step further and I shoot.'

'The time has passed when you could frighten us with such threats. You cannot shoot a whole country, can you? Come on men.'

And Mahadevappa prepared to step on again. The officer's hand went to his belt. Bhima, who had been just behind Mahadevappa, threw himself forward at the same instant as a shot rang out. The next moment, Bhima's huge figure swayed, toppled down, and lay still on the ground. The flag in Mahadevappa's hand wavered. Arvind's hand came out instantly and steadied it. After that, no one moved.

They stood as still as the figure which lay sprawled on the ground. The police officer, his eyes fixed steadily on the men who faced him, his right hand still holding his revolver, gestured with his left hand, holding it above his head, as if beckoning people behind him. Only then did they see them—the lorries parked in the shadows of the trees that bordered the maidan. Armed men in uniforms jumped out and came towards them. The men in the white caps stood motionless and stared at the approaching men expressionlessly.

*

It was not the police, but the Army that had come for the people of Narayanpur this time. By the time they finished, Narayanpur was left desolate. All the prominent men, including old Mahadevappa, had been arrested. It was said that they would be charged with murder and severely punished. Bhima's gymnasium had been burnt. So had Mahadevappa's house and his small press. They had looted most of the houses, including Annu-kaka's.

The house looked bare and entirely strange. This was

not just because so many things had gone, it was Annu-kaka's absence that gave the house its desolate feeling. It was a gloomy and miserable evening. The only light was the lamp before the gods. Timma, who should have lit the lamps, sat in the courtyard, sharing their desolation. The women's eyes were red with weeping. Faces looked at one another in despair. Annu-kaka gone, Sangya gone, Arvind and the others arrested, Bhima dead, Manju lying hurt there—no wonder Amma and the other women looked so shattered. Babu chewed his lips fiercely, wishing there was something he could do.

As if in response, there was a knock at the door. Babu ran to the door, Vasant just behind him. Timma had opened it and was staring out.

'Who is it, Timma?' Babu asked.

'No one,' he said blankly.

'Look,' Vasant pounced on a piece of paper that lay in the doorway. 'There's something here. Someone must have thrown it and run away.' Babu took it from him and both the boys were looking at the piece of paper when Amma came out. 'Who is it?' she asked.

'No one, Amma. But someone seems to have thrown this and gone away.'

'What is it?'

'I don't know.'

'Bring it in, it looks like a letter. Timma, light a lantern.'

Amma opened it and peered at it in the dim light of the oil lamp. 'It's . . . it's from Appa,' she said suddenly in a choked voice.

'Appa?' Manju gasped from her bed.

'Let me see.'

Timma brought in the lantern and placed it near Amma.

'Wait,' Amma's voice was steadier now, 'I'll read it out loud. You can all listen.'

Her voice was steady and low as she read. After the usual

preliminaries, the letter went on, 'So much is happening outside. We hear bits of it and when we do, we chafe at our inactivity here. We long for more news, but it does not always come, nor, when it comes, is it always welcome. We hear of cruel police actions and my heart is heavy that you may have to suffer because of Mohan and me. I am helpless. I cannot help you. Only your own courage can help you to bear it all bravely, complaining as little as possible, and to go on working. I know all of you can do it, even our Babu and Manju.

'But there is hope. I write this not to cheer you or myself, but because I know it is the truth. There is hope. It is an odd thing to say, I know, at such a time when the world is suffering as it has, perhaps, rarely suffered before—when tyrants' boots are marching over poor, defeated lands, when tyrants' hands are snatching away freedom and happiness wherever they can. But this cannot continue. The war will end and when it does, can the world pick itself up and go on the same way again? It cannot. People everywhere are waking out of a long sleep. They will soon find their voices and ask for freedom. And freedom cannot be denied for long to those who are fighting in its name. Not when so many have died for it.

'To us too, freedom will come. And so I say there is hope. I look forward to the day, not far off surely, when we will be together again—free citizens of a free country. Till then we can only go on fighting, shouldering our burdens, however heavy they may be, without complaining.'

Amma came to the end, folded the letter carefully and thoughtfully, staring down at it. There was dead silence.

'I wonder who brought the letter,' Vasant said, breaking the silence at last.

'Some brave hands, undoubtedly,' Amma said and suddenly smiled.

And all the others smiled back. Yes, there were so many brave hands left to go on with the work. Appa was right.

Things would get better. His words brought back hope and courage. They would sit and mope no longer.

'I didn't understand,' Shanti's plaintive voice said. 'Manju-akka, tell me what your Appa wrote in his letter.'

And while Shanti listened to Manju's words, Vasant got up, saying loudly and clearly, 'Come on, Babu, let's light the lanterns. Let's not sit in the dark like this.'

'Yes,' Babu said, getting up himself, 'there's a lot of work to be done.'

Watching the four children, the three women smiled.

Epilogue

IT WAS NOT too long before they came together, as Appa had predicted. Appa was released from jail after he had suffered two years of imprisonment. Mohan too, came out of hiding, when talks of independence had begun and the government decided to become lenient. Mohan, who had become disillusioned with the way the movement had got out of hand, with the wrong kind of people taking over and violence becoming the rule rather than the exception, was only too happy to come home and resume his studies. He did his M.A. and went on to become a journalist. When India became independent on 15 August 1947, they were all together, and watched with pride, joy, and tears in their eyes, the Indian flag being hoisted at midnight.

Annu-kaka was released after a trial of the people of Narayanpur, which became famous throughout the country. Many great lawyers offered their services free to these unfortunate people. Annu-kaka and many others were acquitted as it was clearly proved that they were nowhere around when the incident happened. Arvind and a few others were given stiff sentences, but after independence, they were also released. Arvind went on to become a research scientist, and Babu was one of his best students. Vasant, who shed all his irresponsible ways after Annu-kaka went away, became, like Annu-kaka, a progressive and prosperous farmer. Manju abandoned all ideas of becoming a Rani of Jhansi, and became a doctor instead.

And Shanti, to whom Vasant had once mockingly said, 'Go and write a poem,' surprised him by becoming a good poet after all.

Years later, Shanti wrote of the incident in Narayanpur in a long poem; but, by this time, things had changed so much, that very few people believed it to be true. Nevertheless, it is true, and even today, there is a memorial for Bhima on the maidan at the spot where he fell.

READ MORE IN PENGUIN

In every corner of the world, on every subject under the sun, Penguin represents quality and variety – the very best in publishing today.

For complete information about books available from Penguin – including Puffins, Penguin Classics and Arkana – and how to order them, write to us at the appropriate address below. Please note that for copyright reasons the selection of books varies from country to country.

In India: Please write to *Penguin Books India Pvt Ltd, 706 Eros Apartments, 56 Nehru Place, New Delhi, 110019*

In the United Kingdom: Please write to *Dept. JC, Penguin Books Ltd, Bath Road, Harmondsworth, West Drayton, Middlesex, UB7 ODA, UK*

In the United States: Please write to *Penguin USA Inc., 375 Hudson Street, New York, NY 10014*

In Canada: Please write to *Penguin Books Canada Ltd, 10 Alcorn Avenue, Suite 300, Toronto, Ontario M4V 3B2*

In Australia: Please write to *Penguin Books Australia Ltd, 487 Maroondah Highway, Ring Wood, Victoria 3134*

In New Zealand: Please write to *Penguin Books (NZ) Ltd, 182–190 Wairau Road, Private Bag, Takapuna, Auckland 9*

In the Netherlands: Please write to *Penguin Books Netherlands B.V., Keizersgracht 231 NL–1016 DV Amsterdam*

In Germany : Please write to *Penguin Books Deutschland GmbH, Metzlerstrasse 26, 60595 Frankfurt am Main, Germany*

In Spain: Please write to *Penguin Books S. A., Bravo Murillo, 19-1' B, E-28015 Madrid, Spain*

In Italy: Please write to *Penguin Italia s.r.l., Via Felice Casati 20, I–20124 Milano*

In France: Please write to *Penguin France S. A., 17 rue Lejeune, F–31000 Toulouse*

In Japan: Please write to *Penguin Books Japan, Ishikiribashi Building, 2-5-4, Suido, Tokyo 112*

In Greece: Please write to *Penguin Hellas Ltd, Dimocritou 3, GR–106 71 Athens*

In South Africa: Please write to *Longman Penguin Southern Africa (Pty) Ltd, Private Bag X08, Bertsham 2013*

HEROES NEVER DIE AND OTHER STORIES

Sigrun Srivastava

Some heroes are astonishingly brave, others cowardly and yet others completely crazy, in this exciting collection of stories about ordinary people who are transformed into extraordinary individuals in a crisis. Yet, no matter what feats they are capable of, finally they're all too human—you'll be able to identify with their familiar fears and problems, thrill to their courage and share in their laughter.

'...A good mixture of real life sad stories and lighter ones... a collection of snappy short stories.'

—*Indian Express*

FOR THE BEST IN PAPERBACKS, LOOK FOR THE

INDIAN TALES
Romila Thapar

These tales—of heroes and heroines, their adventures, misfortunes and triumphs; of gods and demons, and of animals—have been told to generations of people who have laughed or shed tears over them or pondered on their timeless wisdom. Some stories have a happy ending, others haunt us with their sadness and all of them should delight the young reader.

An exciting and entertaining collection of stories, full of the colour and enchantment of India.

PANTHER'S MOON
and Other Stories
Ruskin Bond

Ten unforgettable tales of fascinating human encounters with animals and birds—of a man-eater that terrorizes an entire village; a strange and wonderful trust that develops between a fierce leopard and a boy; revengeful monkeys who never forgive a woman who grows dahlias; a crow who genuinely thinks human beings are stupid and many others, creating a world in which men and wild creatures struggle to survive despite each other—a world where, in the end, one is not quite sure which side one is on. A marvellous collection of stories that enchant, amuse and delight.